THE SHRIEKS & THE CREEPS

ANIRBAN GORAI

Contents

CHAPTER I

DISAPPEARED

"You see the new building?"

"Yes?"

"Well, it's haunted."

Sumit still remembered those timid words of Shilpi Dutta. As he sits on his rocking chair beside the mantelpiece, and the fire makes a looming shadow of him behind on the wall, he broods about his school days once again. The photo album is in his weak wrinkled hands and he stares at a picture showing all his friends- Shilpi, Mohit, Rupam, Meena, Ruchi and himself. His eyes go back to the days when they were kids, unknown and careless about the great wide world. All of them were in class 12 when all this happened. Why was he there? He thinks, and curses himself... to be himself. What wrong had he done if he had liked Ruchi and not Shilpi? What wrong was there in sleeping with her? What wrong was there to have friends like Mohit and Rupam? What was their fault? He had lost all them. Surely he was cursed. Yes he was....

A new building was being constructed on the west side of St. Augustine' during those days - a three storey building that would be a well equipped study center with all new facilities, so the then principal Father Richard had said. Not that the school was short of buildings. It already had three buildings respectively for junior, middle and higher classes and two playgrounds that made the school one of the largest schools in sleepy little town of Bokaro, and now this. The structure was almost complete. That day Shilpi had held Sumit's hand and asked him to stay a little while with her after school. Sumit and Ruchi always cycled together to their homes as they were neighbors and he hadn't liked the idea to make his girlfriend wait. But he had to agree when he looked at the pleading face of Shilpi. She asked him if he could help her with some problems, at least for a day Ruchi could cycle alone? Yes, she sure could. Sumit was one of the studious students while Shilpi came under the average section. And moreover, she lived in Gandhi Colony, that was on the other side of the city, quite far from the school as well as Sumit's place, so there were no other means other than school itself to meet Sumit. So after school, he explained Ruchi what he was about to and she had to grumpily leave. Then Sumit had walked up to Shilpi. She was sitting at the edge of the field, on one of the brick benches with her back towards him. Her long shoulder level black hair fell loosely on her back.

"Why don't you tie them up? You will look gentler that way," he said.

"You don't like them loose?" she asked tying her hair in a pony. Then she adjusted her glasses saying, "I thought girls with open hair were the once you liked? Ruchi also keeps her hair that way?"

Sumit had turned away, "if you have called me for this kind of chat, then I am going."

"Wait, wait," she called, "I am sorry."

Reluctantly, he stayed. She brought out the book and showed him her doubts. He explained her with dedication but all the while she kept staring at his face and he knew it. He always felt so awkward the way she stared at him. And so he got up and said, "see, you are not ready for study. Make up your mind because I am not able to concentrate. I will explain you some other day." Only then she had held his wrist and said that the new building was haunted. He had stopped. Then turned and said, "huh? Don't say this to the others. They will laugh at you." And he had jerked off her hand and left.

But it hadn't stopped only at this. This was just the beginning. And Sumit had understood it only when it was way too late. Next day news had spread in the school that the workers at the site had disappeared. Where had they gone, no one knew. All the tools still lay as they were. The manager had gone to check on them when he had found no one. He had tried to call on the team leader's cell phone but there was no response. They hadn't even gone for lunch, because he had waited about two hours for them to return. Then he had told the matter to the principal. Rupam had overheard their conversation while passing by the Principal's office and dutifully conveyed to everyone. There were whispers beginning to go about in the school. Whispers that would change to rumors. And rumours would not be at all good for the school's reputation. So as soon as the Principal learnt about this, he told the students the whole matter during the assembly the next day and then added, "I will go with the manager to file a report at the police station. I request all of you not to go to that building, for if anything bad has happened to them, then it may happen to you all as well. And please remain calm. There's no need to panic."

But! But... they were kids after all. The next day a class 10 student had gone inside the building and had gone missing as well. And how was this known? Viren of class 10 with his friend Rishi, had gone to the building after school the previous day - to find out clues of the missing labourers. Kids at this age can really be something. They watch too many thriller movies and shows and then think they can solve a mystery. This Viren kid had asked Rishi to stay outside and keep a watch so that no one would find them and he gone inside to find clues. Rishi was cross as he wanted to find clues himself. After about an hour he was relieved that he hadn't gone inside with him. When after an hour Viren didn't return, he went in to see. He searched the whole building and could not find his friend. So he went to the principal first thing in the morning and told him the whole matter. Viren's parents were more than panic-stricken than anyone else after hearing what had happened. This news was also conveyed to the students for their safety. There was no question of anyone to even wander around the building anymore.

It was recess and Sumit and group were silently having lunch together when Shilpi had come and broken the silence, "I had told you Sumit, the building is haunted."

"And when did that happen?" Mohit asked, surprised obviously.

"Ah, let it be," Meena said looking at Ruchi's annoyed face.

"Oh, really," Sumit said scornfully, "have you seen the ghost? Then go tell the principal."

"Perhaps I could have seen it, if I had gone there. But what do you have to say about the missing people?" Shilpi said.

There was no explanation. Then Rupam said laughing, "why don't we go and see? Perhaps the ghost will get afraid of the lot of us and return the people?"

"So, this is a joke to you, Mr. Rupam?" Shilpi said staring at him, "you know, how Viren's parents are worried about him?"

Rupam's face fell. "Sorry," he said.

"But Rupam has given us the idea," said Meena, "why don't we go there?"

"You go," said Sumit, "I won't come along."

"We can at least try to find clues," said Shilpi, "or do you really believe in ghosts and are afraid to go there?"

This was enough to start the fire. He stood up and said, "after school,

we all stay and go to the building."

***

Now, what time was it then? Sumit tries to remember. His body and mind has become weak due to age and he keeps forgetting things. Ah... the Class Twelve students completed their classes at two. So it was two then. He along with his group were standing in front of the new building. They had reached it very cautiously without even hinting anyone about it. Richard was strict when it came to rules. And so the lot cautiously reached the site, looking back every now and then in case anyone saw them. The building, though only the structure was done and the interior was still left with spaces for doors and windows to be fitted, looked quiet, sad, lonely and gruesome. Behind the building stood the compound wall and in front of it lay the sprawling ground where kids played during recess or the annual sports day was held. "So, group," said Meena, "what now?"

"We are six," said Sumit, "we shall divide in groups of two and search each storey. We will look for anything unusual." And so the groups were formed. Sumit and Ruchi would search the top floor, Meena and Mohit the lower one and Rupam and Shilpi the ground one. It would be easier for Mohit and Meena because, their floor was about to become a library and so the whole floor was made into one big hall. The groups quickly took their respective floors. The bottom and the top floors were divided into rooms and so it was told to Mohit and Meena if they could not find anything in their floor then they could help others. And so the search began.

Sumit coughs. Old Sumit doesn't have the strength now to think what had happened then. But by and by the scenes come to him again and again. He takes the beer bottle and drinks down a few gulps and rubs his mouth on the sleeve of his shirt. He will turn fifty-eight next month. How old and weak he has become. Yes, he was weaker even then...only he was younger.

About half an hour had passed since the search began and Sumit and Ruchi had looked into most of the rooms. But nothing unnatural or supernatural or unusual was seen. Finally Ruchi said, "I am fed up of all this shit."

"Now, what happened to you?" Sumit said.

"No, you tell me, what has happened to you?" she retorted.

"What do you mean?"

"You like her, don't you?"

"What? Whom?" Sumit was obviously confused. Then it came to him. She was talking of Shilpi. "Oh, no no. Shilpi is just a friend."

"When did I take Shilpi's name?" Ruchi said slyly, "see, you yourself admit it." And she began to walk when he held her wrist.

"After what we have done, how can you say it?" he said.

"I am saying it only after what we have done," she said, "you have changed. You are going towards her."

"Towards whom?" the voice of Shilpi had fallen in their ears and disturbed them in the right time.

"Forget it," said Ruchi and went towards the stairs.

"Where are you going?" Sumit called.

"To the terrace, for some fresh air." And so Ruchi dashed up the stairs, "moreover, your friend has come." This, more sarcastically.

Shilpi kept a hand on his shoulder and said, “she is just disturbed, nothing else.”

“Why are you here?” asked Sumit, “did you look in your floor?”

“Rupam will do it. Only two or three rooms were left. So I came over to help.”

Meanwhile, Mohit and Meena were searching something else. It was a hall they had to look in, and they had done it long ago. Meena had begun staring out of the space that would become a window in future. Mohit joined her too. “Our school looks so beautiful from here,” she said looking at the other buildings.

“I am looking just at you,” Mohit said. They stared at each other for a

while. Then Mohit tried to approach her for a kiss. She giggled and tried to run. But he held her wrist. She giggled again. He giggled too and lifted her to make her sit on the brick base of the open window. Then he brought his lips forward to be touched with hers for a kiss. Some chemistry had been cooking between the two since the chemistry lab in class 10, where they were in the same group. But the proposal had taken some time. Mohit had done it only in the last months of class eleven. And since then they were together.

“Strange, isn’t it?” Sumit said.

“What is strange?” said Shilpi.

“You did your work faster than Mohit and Meena. I mean they had only a hall to look and no one turned up.”

“Oh, I saw them kissing.”

“What? What?” Sumit said as if he hadn’t heard what was said.

“Oh,” said Shilpi, adjusting her glasses, “when I was coming here, I looked on to them and saw they were kissing.”

“Oh, man,” said Sumit, completely annoyed, “they will never understand.”

“By the way,” Shilpi said, shyly, “I had seen you kissing too.”

“What? When?” Sumit was taken aback by the news. He and Ruchi had

kissed several times and it would be very mean of anybody, especially Shilpi to see them.

"Two weeks ago? I had gone to Ruchi's house for a group study. Her parents were not home. The door was not locked. I went in straight away and saw you both in her room."

"Oh, God," was only what Sumit could say.

"I ran away then," she continued. There was a pause. Then again she said slowly, "so...did you...I mean...did the two of you do it?"

This came as another explosion to Sumit. "What?"

"I mean...the conditions were perfect, there was no one home. So did you two make it? I mean did you...do it...I mean...?"

"Shilpi?" Sumit almost shouted, "be quiet, enough. You have said enough and seen enough. Please. Oh God, you..."

Of course they had done it. He knew her parents would be out that day and she had called him to teach her Math. Math was just a reason. And he had understood it quite well and so he had not forgotten to take the safety measures along.

Sumit said, "you know, she thinks I like you."

"But you don't," said Shilpi, going to the vacant space of the wall, "but I like you, and you know that."

Sumit's face went red with blushing. He knew she liked him but had not said this before so clearly. He looked away from her staring eyes and said, "Let's continue the search."

Meanwhile, Rupam looked quite flustered. 'Man, where is everybody,'

he thought, 'I have looked in the whole building and no one. Like whoosh...everyone has just vanished?'

It was very late...very... Sumit broods. But Rupam was not confused, neither had he turned insane. He actually was not able to find anyone in the building. And when after about half an hour he had exhausted all his energy he sat down on the floor itself and began thinking his mates had actually vanished like the others. But then, he saw someone standing in front of him. That someone told him that not his mates, but it was he who had vanished from their lives.

"Okay, now let's see the terrace as well," Sumit had said and was about to go upstairs when Meena came shrieking.

"What happened Meena? Why are you crying?" Shilpi asked. But Meena kept hiccupping and sobbing. She was extremely terrified. Sumit kept his palm on her shoulder and asked, "where's Mohit?"

"Vanished," she said.

"Calm down, and say what really happened, will you?" said Shilpi.

Meena said, "we both were sitting by the wall when...when he vanished."

"Vanished? Like what?" said Sumit, certainly not understanding what was being said.

"Vanished means vanished, you idiot," Meena almost screamed, "just whoosh...like that, in thin air. You have seen the serials of Gods? How they appear and disappear? One moment he was there happily chatting and the next he wasn't. I just turned my head slightly to see what he was trying to show me outside the window. I turned to see him again and he was gone. He wasn't there. I am telling you, there is something in here." Then she began crying again.

"What the hell's happening?" said Sumit and ran for the stairs. As he began going down, he saw Ruchi coming from the terrace. "What happened?" she asked.

"Ask them," said he and ran down the stairs. Ruchi walked up to the girls to know what was going on.

Sumit searched the whole floor, then the lower one too. He found nothing. Neither Mohit, nor Rupam. All he could find were the tools of the labourers that were left behind. He tried to call them, but there was always a busy tone on their numbers. Reluctantly, he had to return. Meena was quiet now. He walked up to them and told about the two missing. This sent Meena crying again. "Now what will happen?" asked Ruchi. All Sumit thought was that how could anyone disappear just like that. According to Meena, Mohit had vanished just like that, like a ghost in a horror movie. And what about Rupam? What about the others?

"I am going out of here," Meena had suddenly cried and began walking for the stairs with fast steps when Shilpi had held her by her wrist.

"Look, we must think calmly," she said.

"Shilpi's right," so said Sumit glancing at the annoyed face of his girlfriend, "Don't go berserk."

"You all are going berserk," Meena cried, "Rupam and Mohit have vanished. We all will too. Can't you see that? I am not staying here any longer."

"And what if they are in danger? What if something has happened to them? Will you leave your best friends in danger?" Sumit's harsh words had silenced everyone for a while.

Then Meena said, "you haven't seen him disappear Mr. Sumit Verma. Or you would have not talked so bravely." The tears from her eyes had now dried off.

Sumit sighed and said, "I will not go without finding my friends. Not till I get even the slightest hint about what actually has happened here. If you all are afraid, then you are free to go."

Sumit now broods what on Earth had made him said this. He had been really berserk. He should have left the place first thing. But he stayed. And so had stayed Shilpi. Ruchi was with Meena. She asked for the final time if he would come. He had shaken his head. She had taken a deep breathe and left, holding Meena by her shoulder. He turned only when the two girls had turned round the corner and were out of sight. But he saw Shilpi smiling. "And what on Earth makes you smile?" he asked.

"Now, it's just you and me," she said and approached him for a kiss.

But Sumit pushed her off, "Shilpi, you are my friend. Don't cross your limits."

"They will disappear too," her words fell as a threatening in his ears and then he saw the smile on her face – a cruel smile. Her eyes too, that shined in jet black. An unknown fear made him run towards the stairs. But when he came down he could see no one. The girls were not there, neither outside the building nor inside. He called on their numbers too, but same as Rupam and Mohit, he got a busy tone on their cell phones as well. He knew they had disappeared too. He returned to Shilpi. She was still standing there, smiling. "I told you," she shrugged.

"Why do I feel that you knew all this would happen?" he asked.

"You can get them back," she said and looked across the hall. Suddenly, there stood all his friends- Rupam, Mohit, Meena, Ruchi and Viren too. Only the workers were missing. Everything was going like a whirlwind in Sumit's head. He felt his head would explode. He ran up to them and asked, "what happened?"

"It's like another dimension. People coming here into this building, vanish and can never be seen again," said Rupam, "I came to know this when I thought you all had disappeared and then Viren here came to me from nowhere. He said it was me who had vanished and not you all. He said if we vanish, we won't be seen, neither would we be able to communicate with others. For some time I couldn't see you all, but then after an hour you all were visible but couldn't

hear us however much we called."

"It's like an... like an invisible jail," came from Ruchi with welled up eyes.

"But now you are okay, you all have returned," said Sumit when Shilpi began laughing. How foolish he was. And this he realized when winds began to howl in the hall from nowhere. Shilpi's hair stood floating and her eyes turned black fully. Her grin told him she was responsible for all of this.

"Why? Shilpi? Why?" he cried.

"Not because I was teased every day in school for being a weirdo, not because I couldn't get the boy I liked, not because the boy I loved, loved someone else, not because he slept with her too, not because he didn't accept my love," she said, her voice echoing in the whole building, "but because this is fun." And with a simple twist of her palms, the group disappeared from in front of the very eyes of Sumit. And all he could do was to watch helplessly. All was calm within seconds. He grabbed Shilpi by her shoulders and asked, "how did you do this, witch? How could you do this?"

She jerked him off, "all your life now you shall think about me and no one else. You will see how I make your life miserable. Witch? Huh? Now you recognize me well." And so she melted away with the air too. As if there was no Shilpi Dutta, standing and laughing there. Only he stood in the whole building.

Disappearance of so many kids together was too much for the school, and so the plan for a new centre was held up for good. The new building of St. Augustine's was never completed. People didn't go anywhere near it again. Two or three tried, and yes they returned safely, but terrified. They said they could hear whispers within the halls. Whispers of children. The building still stands there, quiet, alone, sad and gruesome.

After that event Sumit had gone on leave. Seeing all that happening before his eyes had taken the better of him and he had fallen ill. He only thanked God he hadn't lost his sanity after what had happened. When he returned he got to know that she had left and gone to another city, where to, no one knew. Sumit even went to see her at her house, but there was no one there. The flat owner (she obviously lived on rent) also didn't know where they had gone. But Shilpi was true in her words. All his life Sumit feared she would return from that day when all that happened. She never contacted him again. But he didn't marry, as he feared she would return and make his life miserable. All his life he has remained alone, aloof from everyone. He looks at the album again and smiles. She was right, he had thought about her all his life. After all, he felt guilty, in a way he was responsible for his friends. All he does now, is wait. He waits for her to return. To come back for him and give him a silent and peaceful death. He knows she is there somewhere and watching him. And he is ready to welcome her.

****

CHAPTER II

THE FINAL TASK

Oh so many years have passed, I can't clearly remember now. Those days were the days of my struggling. Only a month had passed since Sitarampur had seen my fortunate feet upon itself and I was intensely involved into getting my same unstable feet stable somehow. Only a few years had passed since the setting up of the plant and it required men. So I had decided to get myself a job there. My father had only said this, "good for you, now at least you will do something in life." But as destiny would have it, I didn't get a job immediately. Before that I was to come across an incident that was going to leave me dumbfounded. An event that was surely beyond human wit and intelligence.

I along with my two other friends had taken a flat on rent which belonged

to a person from our own village who worked as a teacher in the primary school here. He was on vacation for a month and my father had arranged for my stay at his abode. Since he was going for such long duration, he decided that giving his flat at rent to a known person would suffice for two things – firstly protection from thieves and secondly he could make extra cash also. So he had given his flat to us at a minimal cost. Ranjan and Gaurav, my friends, were both trying their hands at getting a job at the plant. Apart from that, we had also run for the CISF inductions and failed. Gaurav was pursuing a correspondence degree in B.ED as well. That time, day in and day out, our only work was to eat, sleep, and roam. Sitarampur had only started to be civilized, so there was not much to see in it. You can say, we have seen the town grow in front of our eyes.

The event happened to begin on one such occasion when my friends were away on their respective ventures and I had gone to the local market. I had heard it was the city's largest vegetable market that sold old items as well. Anything ranging from clothes to books, the later being my field of interest. So after a good research about it, I decided to give it a visit. Since I had no other work and I am very much into reading, I could pass my time happily. So I was there at around three in the afternoon. There were very less means of travel those days so I had to walk most of the distance. Although the market was only three kilometers from the place I lived. I like spending time all by myself and I soon became very much involved into all the hustle and bustle of the market place. So many people, with the smells of the different cuisines in the stalls, I forgot all for a few moments. It was then that I saw him staring at me.

The boy was about same age as mine. He stood beside a meat shop and his dress-up of an old brown shirt and a pair of barmundas said he belonged from the same area. His hair was matted and he was skinny. At any moment he seemed a part of the crowd and I would not have even looked at him. What set him apart from the others was how intently he stared at me. First I thought he was looking at someone else but then very soon I realized that it was me he was staring at. First I thought to ignore him and put my concentration on other things, but when I passed by him and crossed him even, I could clearly feel his eyes set upon me, moving along with my movement.

At other times I would have stopped and asked –'why brother, what's the matter?' but not today. There was this eerie feeling about him that was sending chills up my back. Why, I don't know, but I decided to ignore him totally. But when I crossed him and after walking around 100 or so steps ahead turned to see whether he was still there, yes sir, there he stood staring at me with his cold black eyes, at his own old position, not moved an inch. I put away my eyes and decided to continue my venture.

It was around seven when I decided to return. I had my fill, moving in the book market, admiring all the books. Though I didn't buy any. I already had two books left to finish and I thought buying more would only increase the burden. I was heading towards the main road when I had to stop short at my place. The same boy from the afternoon was standing again, right there across the road in front of a betel shop, his eyes set upon me with glue. Though I was quite far from him, still I knew he was staring at me only. I didn't want any worries on my head. There were already too many. I just shrugged off the matter, looked other side and took an auto-rickshaw. But there was something about him that didn't let me forget him. Whole night I kept dreaming about him. His eyes always locked on me.

***

A couple of days passed. I didn't get to go towards Market for some time and so I didn't see that strange fellow again. I had almost forgotten him now. One evening I was returning after eating samosas when something happened that left me stunned. As I mentioned already, there was not much in the city to venture for, and though there were houses, the place seemed quite vacant for the less number. During those days, most people had lands to eat from, and a job would only be the more reason to be penalized. Even I had to fight at home to do a job. Doing a job for people like us was a sin. So the city didn't have people in it. The plant needed labour as well but to bring in labour you have to keep things ready, isn't it. Quarters to live in, hospital, schools - you have to get things done before hand, even if you have only half the labour with you. So the samosawala also put his stall a kilometer away from my building, so that the whole of the area could come under his jurisdiction. I had taken a shortcut for my room through some narrow and congested alleys so I could reach faster. Clouds had covered the sky and the wind was strong. It would rain anytime. I was taking fast paces when I felt somebody behind me. First I didn't give much attention to it. Thought somebody else was in a hurry too. It was seven and now it was almost dark. It would take me another five minutes to reach my room. I could feel how fast the person behind me was walking so I took the side of the dusty alley for him to pass. But he didn't. He just kept behind me with the same fast paces. I shrugged and began walking again. Then something got into me and a shiver ran up my spine on the thought that the person behind was following me.

This thought came to me on the observation that there was no one else tonight on the road. Why? I couldn't guess. I didn't dare to look back. I just walked on. But I had to decide whether I was really being followed or it was just a whim of my brain. I slowed down my steps. The person behind me also slowed down. Then I increased my speed a little. The same was copied. Suddenly I could feel a few drops on my face. It was beginning to rain. I increased my paces. My room was very near now. Just a hundred steps more. My follower increased his speed too. I didn't even know whether the follower was a 'he' or a 'she'. But I knew this that he/she was following me. When I reached the alley where my block was just at the corner, I decided to take a look at my follower. I was stunned to see there was no one.

Where did he go? How? Could have he turned at the first corner itself? Must have. I decided, no one can vanish just like that in thin air. He must have turned at the previous alley. My room was on the ground floor itself so I had to just work on the lock to get in. I had just opened the door and put my left foot inside when my eyes went over to my right side and I almost slipped. The door helped me save myself. The same boy from the Market was standing there wearing the same old clothes, with his same old cold eyes, staring at me. I went in and closed the door. Took four heavy breathes. Then thought, this was not done. This little fellow was frightening the shit out of me for no reason. What would he do to me? I thought. Couldn't I handle one person, that too someone who looked a lot younger than me? I opened the gate to talk to him and was literally shocked to see him gone. He was nowhere. I realised, perhaps it was him only in the alley also.

***

A couple of days more passed. But I could not put that boy away from my head. I was confused. Why? Was all that moved round my head. Why does he stare at me that way? Why was he following me? Did he want to say something? If so, then why didn't he talk that day? What did he want from me? Or was it just that he was playing a prank on me with his friends? And if so, then why was only I being the prey? When I thought and thought till I began feeling that my brain would pop out of my head and didn't get any result, I decided to find the boy out. And I went to the market once again.

I looked all around, and very carefully, looking at every corner, every shop, every stall and every gathered crowd. But I couldn't find the boy. I asked about him at almost all the shops but they knew nothing. I asked at the shop where I had seen him as well, I asked whether some boy worked there or not, but they knew about no one. They thought I was some mad man. I worked hard all afternoon. Towards the evening I sat down at a small park near the market, all tired and exhausted. I decided to sit there for some time, watch the greenery (and mind you I am not talking about the trees) around and then return. But I had not realized that it was going to be a long stay in the area. I saw the boy staring at me from behind a tree.

First, I thought it was someone else, I couldn't make out clearly as he was behind some bushes. But then he came out in the open and showed himself. I decided I would get him today and I called out to him. To my surprise, he didn't say anything nor did he come towards me. Instead he turned away. "Hey, you," I called again and this time he began walking - away from me. I got up and began to follow him. I had to finish the matter today - anyhow. It was becoming unbearable for me. I walked behind him.

He walked slowly. First I thought I could run and catch him. But then it came to me that if he really wanted me to catch him, then he would have easily done it the day he was following me. He could have talked to me that day. He didn't want me to catch him, he wanted me to follow him. So I did as he wanted. I followed him but kept at a safe distance.

He went out of the park and began walking towards the residential area, that was to be called as sector 2. I was surprised to see that when it came to crossing roads, he didn't even look for any vehicles, not that there were not any to be afraid of. He just walked as if the road was his father's and no one would hit him, and it was even greater surprise that he really didn't get hit. I let the matter go and just followed him. Very soon he turned at a corner and took a lonely alley.

Within minutes I saw him walk inside a three-storied building. I followed. I was in the first floor when I saw him enter a flat in the second floor. The door was open from before and he pulled it shut as he entered. That's it, I thought, he wanted me to follow. I triumphantly hurried up the rest of the stairs and pushed the door thinking it to be unlocked. But it wouldn't budge. I saw the doorbell and pressed it two times. Inside the Mrityunjay Mantra began ringing instead of bell. One of those fancy bells, I thought. A woman opened the door, who possibly looked like the maid. "Yes?" she asked.

"I ...er...ah," came out my mouth, I couldn't decide what to say. I knew no one in this house, and what would I say, 'the boy of this house had been following me?' But to my relief the woman called someone saying, "Babuji, someone's here to see you," and she went away gesturing me to get in. I followed her into a hall.

"Who is it?" came an old shaky voice and presently an old man in his late seventies entered the hall from one of the rooms. He walked by the help of a stick and wore dhoti, a long shirt and big glasses. He had very little hair and a thick moustache. "I ..er.. I ," came again from my mouth and this time, to my greatest surprise the old man grasped my hand and said, "Rohan, you came at last."

I was bewildered for the moment. I mean how could an old man, whom I didn't even know to exist, knew me so well. He pulled me by the hand saying, "why are you standing here in the heat?" and taking me into one of the rooms, made me sit on the sofa. Then he called the maid to provide some refreshments at once and switched on the fan himself. "I ... I think you are mistaken, I came here...," I began but my words were cut short by the old man's words. As if he wasn't listening to me. He said, "it has been a long time since I talked with Mukesh, how is he? How are your parents?" I was stunned to hear my father's name from his mouth. This matter was getting even more interesting. But I couldn't say anything. I didn't have anything to say. But the matter had to be cleared. So I said firmly, "look, sir, there has been a mistake. You are mistaking me for someone else. I don't even know you."

The old man looked at me with questioning eyes for a moment. There was silence for a few seconds. Then he took off his glasses, rubbed them on his shirt and wore them again. Finally he sighed and went over to the big old wooden almirah at one of the corners of the room. He opened the door with a creek and took out a large photo album. He then dusted off the dirt and handed it to me. As it is, I was confused already with the events going on, I took the album and began turning the pages. I was shocked to see the photos - there was a very younger version of me, my family, my uncles, aunts, cousins - everyone I knew in my family. I looked at the old man once and then again at the photos, then again at the old man. And every time my eyes went wide with amazement. There was this old man too in the photos. These photographs ranged from different occasions - marriage, family photos, some were even from different tours. Now the big question - what was my relation with this old man? But I didn't have to ask. He answered himself. He said, "I am Narendra Choudhary, your paternal grandfather's younger brother. I will be your grandpa."

Even in a trance, the etiquettes didn't leave me. I at once knelt forward and touched my new grandpa's feet. He touched my head for blessings. I sat again. The maid brought tea and samosas and put them on the table. "Eat," grandfather said. I hesitantly took one. "Now, tell me," he began, "how did you find this place? Your father told you?"

I shook my head, "no, he...in fact no one has ever told me about you before. I told you, I didn't even know you when I came here. I was following this boy who entered this house."

"Boy?" Grandpa said, surprised, "which boy?"

I told him the whole story of the boy stalking me, and how I followed him here. This came as a great surprise to my listener. Finally he said, "but there is no boy in this house, son."

There had to be some mistake, I decided. The words of my host rang again and again in my ears. No boy in this house, how could that be possible? The old man said, "why would I lie, son? There is no boy that you are talking about."

I gave a glance all around the house. Every room of the flat was open

and one could see the whole flat at one glance. There really was no boy. The album was still open on my lap. I just gave a look at one of the photos and there among the people stood the same boy, in the same clothes, smiling. "Here," I said excitedly turning the album towards grandpa and pointing at the picture, "this boy, you see?"

The old man took the album and gave a serious look at the picture. For a few moments he said nothing. Then he stood up and said, "what you are saying is impossible, son. Come with me." And he held my wrist once again. I followed him in one of the rooms. This room was smaller than the others and only a cot lay in it. It seemed like the maid slept here. He pointed at the wall. There was a photo with flowers around it. It was of the same boy who had been turning off my sleeps since so many days. Grandpa said, "the boy you are talking about is Somesh, and he passed away a year and a half ago."

***

The words still felt like melted glass in my ears. How could this be possible? A dead boy - stalking me, whom I followed and reached here. What was happening? At once I felt like this was some reality show where someone was making the fool out of me by playing a very big prank. But no, this wasn't the truth, and I understood that. My new grandfather told me Somesh's story. He was the maid's son and had come with his mother four years ago to work for him. They lived here itself with him. As no one was left in Narendra's life so he allowed them to live with him and do all the work, and he would pay them well. Somesh used to do small odd jobs - like bringing eggs, bread, bringing water, like that. The main thing was he was going to the government school as well. He had a thing for books and grandpa had money. He thought as the maid - Kamla, was doing all the household tasks, then why should his son be pressed into the same. So he began sending him to the nearby government school.

But in living here with the old man, the boy grew a great likeness and respect for him. He listened to every instruction he gave like an obedient son. Narendra also grew very fond of him. There was only one thing that worried him and which was his last wish. He hadn't talked to his brother or with any of the family members in years. The story went that, Narendra had some major row with his elder brother, i.e. my grandpa Mahendra and had left village with his wife years ago. The main reason why I didn't know about him. Because grandpa had told everyone not even remember him, surely he had done something really grave. Whatever it was I didn't ask the reason. I was more interested in the story.

So my new grandpa came to Sitarampur with his wife. They couldn't have any children. So the couple lived a forlorn and solitary life in this town. They grew old, and grandma left him as well. Then Kamla came with his son. She was from our village itself and she had come to Sitarampur in search of work. She came to my new grandpa and this old man helped her out. When egos clash, relationships die. The two brothers never talked to each other in all these years. So when Narendra became really lonely, his last wish came to be that he could talk with his family, moreover with his brother even once. Grandpa was no more, so his only wish was to see even any one of the family members. He had told this to Somesh. In the two years or so, he had become like a son to him and Narendra had shared all with him. Now as he stared at Somesh's portrait and completed the story, I saw a drop of tear at the corner of his eye. Kamla was at the door, listening to everything.

"But... grandpa, I am sure, the boy I am talking about was he," I said.

"Somesh was a weak fellow son," Kamla said, "he suffered with jaundice three times. Couldn't go through the last attack. Poor fellow, he suffered

a lot. How can he come to you, son?"

I began to look down. I had no answer to this. But Narendra Choudhary had. He said, "he wanted to fulfill my wish, Kamla. I had told him I wanted to meet my family. Wanted to see any one of them, wanted to hug them and see, Rohan is here. He took my last wish as his own and see, he completed his final task."

Kamla's eyes filled with tears. I couldn't stop my eyes from watering as well. This event, though confusing even now, was clear like water.

With this Rohan finished his story. The kids listened to their father with their mouths wide open. "What happened after that?" asked little Meena. Rohan paused. "Tell na, what happened after that?" said Tarun.

"After that my children..." said Rohan lifting Meena up on his lap, but he couldn't complete his words. Because a more hoarse voice interrupted, "after that I came home." Old Narendra Choudhary stood at the door with his stick and smiled. Both the kids cried 'dadaji' and ran for him laughing. Narendra also laughed. "Your father brought me and Kamla back here," he said, "and we became to little happy family." Then the kids' mother called them for dinner and they hopped away inside. The old man sat on the bed. "Twelve years have passed since the incident," said Rohan, "I still can't believe it happened."

"Some things happen," said the old man, looking at Somesh's portrait, "yet remain unexplainable. Somesh is one of them."

****

CHAPTER III

JOHAR

The four storeyed hotel stood at one part of the Main Market. The west of the sprawling market place had been kept for such bigger agendas as a result of which, two four storied hotels stood majestically here. The first one, Hotel Riya is not of our concern. The story is about the second one, Hotel Johar. The building looked magnificent from a distance, with its large parking space and 10 feet compound surrounding it. Being one of the most luxurious hotels in the town, it kept its own facilities from ATM to great fooding. Though this is rear in a small town like Shyamnagar.

It was the month of July. The young couple had checked into Johar in the evening. The long sultry journey in the train from Bhilai had drained the couple completely. Vivek Mathur was an engineer at the factory here, and had been sent here for some assignment. This would be a work-cum-holiday trip for them so he brought along his wife as well. He had decided he would complete his survey by two days, and then he would take Priya sight-seeing. He had been to this town before on business, but it was three years ago. There would be much to see here now. Right now, Vivek lay on the bed waiting for Priya to come out of the washroom. Priya came out alright, but her dress-up suggested the time was right for some mischiefs. She wore a white thigh-length night gown with one of the straps falling down from her shoulder over her arm. Her wet back-level hair fell loosely behind and Vivek knew her intentions from her eyes. The windows were open and a cool breeze ignited the fires within them. Without losing time, Vivek picked his wife in his arms and laid her on the bed. She giggled as he kissed her all over her face and arms. Then, remembering to put on protection he said, "just give me a minute" and hurried into the bathroom.

Priya sat up and began straightening her hair. Then, feeling a little thirsty she headed for the table that already had a glass and a jug of water. But when she

picked up the jug and looked inside, she had to put it back at its place. There was no water in it, though it had something else. It was of darker colour and seemed more condensed. She dipped a finger inside and when she took it out she could clearly see that the liquid was red and smelled like blood. Horrified, she sat back on the bed.

"I am back," Vivek said coming out of the washroom, "I don't think my lady had to wait long." He headed for the glass of water for a drink. "No, don't," came out of Priya's mouth, but till then he had taken a sip of the water. "Why?" asked Vivek, obviously surprised. Priya's mouth dropped open when she saw little water droplets at the corners of his lips. She came up to him and looked into the glass. Water. What had she seen then at first? Was the journey getting to her brain? May be? She sat back with her fingers on her head. "What's the matter?" asked Vivek, sitting beside her, concerned, "something wrong?"

"I think I am tired," said Priya.

"Then you should sleep," said Vivek, "go on, take a nap."

"No," said she, "if I rest now, I won't get sleep at night, you know that."

"Who said we would sleep at night?" said Vivek. Priya smiled staring at him. He winked with his mischievous eyes. She kept her head on his shoulder. He lovingly wrapped his hands around her. He knew something was wrong. "Okay, I have a better idea," said Vivek, "let's go out somewhere."

They returned late at night after going around shopping. Dinner would be

given at the hotel itself. So they had to just get into the room and lie down on the bed. Priya did so, Vivek went in to take a shower before the food would come. Priya began humming a tune while playing with her locks when suddenly she heard something. The sound came right into her ears, though it was not clear. She sat up and tried hard to listen carefully. And just as she did so, suddenly her eyes went wide with horror and chills ran up her neck.

"You shouldn't have come here."

The voice was almost a whisper but very clear now. She could also make out that it was a female voice. She looked around, opened the door to look outside, even opened the balcony but who could be found there? Vivek came out of the bathroom and saw his wife sitting on the bed looking frantically here and there. She perspired profusely. "Hey, love," he said, "what happened?"

"There's someone," she said, "there's someone in this room."

"What are you saying?" asked Vivek, obviously confused, "there is no one here but the two of us."

But Priya could hear the whispers right in her ears. "You shouldn't have come here. Now it is time for payback." A horrified Priya looked at Vivek, then around the room, but could find no possible source of the voice. Suddenly there was sound of metal cracking. And before anyone could guess, the fan came down right upon Priya's head, throwing blood at a horrified Vivek's face.

***

It was midnight. Vivek wept as the hotel manager tried to calm him down, offering water which he denied thrice now, while the police looked for clues. The body of Priya with a thrashed head lay on the bed, with the bed sheet wet with blood, while the fan lay just beside her. A photographer clicked his instrument continuously. "What you are saying is totally absurd Mr. Mathur," said Inspector Sunil Rai. The muscularly built officer of the local police station was new in town and a total atheist. "You are saying that your wife was hearing things," he continued, "what was she hearing actually? Can you explain? Because there were only you two in the room and we have checked the whole place and we got nothing."

"I don't know," said Vivek, "I don't know what she was hearing. Just that I had never seen her so afraid before. She was all sweaty...I could see the fear in her face when she was looking here and there.... and then suddenly the fan came down..."

One constable took a stool and stood on it to check the hook on which the fan was hanging. He came down and reported, "I cannot see any effect there."

"See? I told you there could not be a problem in our work," said the manager facing the inspector.

"Then how did the fan fall Mr. Yashwant?" asked Sunil in a rough tone, "or is it that you are just making up a story Mr. Vivek?"

"What do you mean?" Vivek stood up surprised.

"I mean, your wife was in the bathroom when you loosened the bolts of the fan and when she came out you made her sit on the bed, where the fan fell on her, battering her head. Nice way to make it look like an accident, huh?"

Vivek's face boomed with anger. He grabbed at the inspector's collar almost screaming, "so you think I killed my wife, huh?"

Sunil removed his hands and said, "just stay calm Mathurji or I can arrest you on charges of assaulting an officer on duty." Vivek sat on the bed and burst into tears again. "The matter seems a little strange. You are not allowed to leave the city until all is clear." And then collecting all evidences that could be found, including the fan and the body, the police left.

***

Inspector Sunil sat at his table with his head scratching. His cap lay on the table. He ordered for a glass of water and began thinking. He was a sharp officer, good at his work. But his honesty had led him to more transfers than promotions. Shyamnagar was his fourth in his 8 years of service. He had been here only eight months and this was the first murder case he had got. Finally, some action, he thought. The sound of the constable entering his room brought him back from his thoughts. As the constable put the water on his table, he asked him, "this hotel Johar has seen deaths before, isn't it?"

"Yes sir," the constable said, "why do people go there I don't understand. That hotel has seen many deaths in its small life of nine years. Don't people find out where they are going?"

"And why is the place still running?"

"They are rich people, sir. Money can do wonders and moreover, all the

deaths were just accidents, so nothing could be proven out."

This made the inspector think even harder. The constable was asked to bring the hotel's file. Putting it on the desk, he drowned himself into it.

Vivek stood in the balcony with the support of the hand railings. Tears were dry now, but the scene was not. Priya's gory body remained in front of his eyes all the time. It was already 9 and he hadn't slept the whole night. Suddenly, he heard the sound of breaking glass and saw the glass of water on the floor, in pieces. He came in and knelt down to pick the pieces when he heard another sound. But this one was not of breaking glass. It was of door banging. Someone was knocking at the door so hard, it seemed the person other side would break it down. "Who's it?" Vivek asked out loud. But no answer came. The banging continued. "Oh, for God's sake, I am coming," said Vivek irritated and went up to the door. He opened it, only to see no one. He looked all along the corridor, but there was no one. What's happening? He thought. Only a moment ago someone was desperate to get in and now there is no one. He closed the door.

He turned to get to his previous work when the banging began again. Perspiration emerged on Vivek's forehead. Fear gripped him. He opened the door again, and again there was no one. He closed the door and came and sat on the bed. "What's happening?" he murmured. And then those cold whispering words fell in his ears - 'you shouldn't have come here.' Vivek began looking all around like a mad man. His body drenched with sweat. "Who are you?" he shrieked. But would there be any answer. The whispers came again after a moment's silence. 'You should not have come here. See, what happened to your wife.' Bewildered, he picked up the receiver of the phone to call the room service. But there was no answer. He tried to run out of the room but the door wouldn't open, however much he tried. Finally he ran to the balcony. But in running, the glass pieces pierced into his feet. He limped, shrieking, but did not stop.

The pain made him kneel down to pick out the glass pecks. He held the railings for support. Blood gushed out of his wounds. 'See what you have done to yourself,' the voice came again. He looked here and there with fear. Suddenly the iron rods came off and he fell head long to the cemented ground.

***

Inspector Sunil didn't have to go up to the third floor where Vivek's room was, to meet him. He found his dead body on the ground itself, with crowd gathered around it. He looked at the broken iron railings of the balcony and told his assistants to do the necessary procedure, then went in to meet the manager. The manager was at the reception with the other colleagues. "Oh, so finally someone called you," said Yashwant as soon as he saw the cop.

"I came to tell Mr. Mathur that he was clear of his wife's case," said Sunil, "but what do you mean by that?"

"Oh?" said Yashwant, sounding surprised, "so no one called you. You came on your own?"

The inspector nodded. The manager said, "and I thought someone's cell phone finally caught signal and you were called. We found the body fifteen minutes ago and since then we have been trying to call you. But surprisingly none

of the persons in this hotel was having any signal on his or her phone. Isn't that strange?"

This made the cop's face grim. Then the manager asked why did he think that Vivek was clear. So the inspector explained why. Reading the file on Hotel Johar, he found out that there had been nine murders in the past nine years, one in each. And all of the murders had happened in strange circumstances. Very simple accidents had caused the victims serious head injuries leading to their instant deaths. Like, the first one had slept in the bathroom and his head had been hit at the bath tub's corner, leading to his spot death. Second one had fallen off the stairs leading to a grave wound on his forehead. And so on and so forth. There had not been proofs that would show they had been murders. So death of Priya by the fan was sort of same. And now Vivek was gone as well. And he too had injury in his head.

"So what do we do now?" asked Yashwant.

"Now, we search the whole hotel," declared Sunil.

"What? But why?" asked Yashwant, astounded, "there is no reason to check..." Then seeing the grim face of the cop he said, "I mean, they are all accidents, right? There's no proof they had been murdered..."

"So why is it your hotel always? From the last nine years? Why do all the people die in your hotel only? Just beside you, the Riya stands. It didn't see blood yet? Or is it that people love to die in your hotel?"

The manager had no answers to the questions of the cop. He just looked at his face and then to the floor then again to his face. The officer's serious face gave him the creeps. He said finally, "so what is it you want to search?"

Sunil had called a search party for his unofficial search and they would be here any moment now. Of course he had to urge his seniors quite some time for it. By then he and Yashwant sipped coffee at the table, discussing their next course of action. He had ordered Yashwant not to tell the owner of the hotel Mr. Raman about any of this. He didn't want a rich person like him to get disturbed, he said. "Let him sit back in Kolkata and enjoy his vacation," Sunil said. But personally, the cop felt that the owner somehow had very grim sides associated with this hotel's past. The thing was, this hotel had been built over an older smaller hotel about nine years ago. That hotel's owner had been given a lucrative price for his hotel and then it was demolished. Hotel Johar was born after that. Sunil actually thought he could find something among the walls of this place. He was 60 percent confident.

Very soon the search party arrived and the inspector gave directions about searching the whole building. When asked what was being looked for, he just said - 'anything that is suspicious and related to death.' Then he made Yashwant request the people of the hotel to remain calm and co-operate with the search. It was just a routine check. While the rest of the party did its work - going in every room and searching everything from bags to toilets,

Sunil took Yashwant straight to the top floor. Yes, there were other officers as well, but his target was a special room. Room no. - 043. Why? Because according to his search, 3 out of the nine deaths had happened in this room.

Room - 043 was locked. It was vacant since the past one week. Yashwant opened the lock and both got in. The room smelled of dirt from within. "You didn't get this room cleaned?" asked the officer. "I would," said Yashwant, "just in a day or two."

Sunil went to the large window across the room and looked outside. The whole of the sprawling Main Market could be seen from here. Just beside the window was the door to the balcony that was also locked. What actually had happened nine years ago and that Sunil hadn't mentioned to Yashwant was that the owner, Santosh Lal, of the earlier hotel in place of which Johar was now standing had disappeared just a few days after the inauguration of the new hotel and his body whether dead or alive had never been found since then.

So, there might have been actually ten murders in the last nine years, instead of nine, Sunil reasoned. Because there hadn't been any research for him really? A report had been taken down - 'missing for the last three days. Dated - 12th July 2005'. Surely, it had been murder and the matter had been silenced by money. Another thing was that the deceased had been last seen in this hotel only, and in the same room where Sunil now stood, before getting disappeared.

He opened the door and came into the balcony. Since it was nine years ago, so getting any kind of witness to testify the disappearance of Santosh now would not be possible. There was a name in the report but the sharp inspector knew it would be a fake person even before his assistants brought news about him. So, he decided a little search might get him somewhere on this case. He looked all around him. Nothing unusual. Yashwant came up to him. Suddenly, the cop felt as if someone breathed air in his ears. He turned towards Yashwant who stood behind him. Why would he do such a childish act? Then thinking it to be a conduct of the air, he started to say something when the breathing came again. He looked all around him. "What's that you are looking at?" The words falling on his eardrums were crystal clear. Sunil looked at Yashwant suspiciously but knew he wasn't the one doing it. What was it then? Hallucination? "You are looking at the wrong place," the whisper came again. Afraid of any mishappening, Sunil hurriedly got into the room and sat on the bed.

"So what are you searching here, officer?" asked Yashwant coming up to him. Sunil decided to pay attention to the case when he heard a creaking sound. He looked up and saw the fan swinging to and fro. At first, Sunil didn't give attention to it, but then, the thought that the cause of Priya's death was a fan made him jump to his feet. He asked Yashwant, "do the fans of your hotel swing often?"

"Oh, it must be the wind's doing," suggested Yashwant. But Sunil knew it was not the wind's work. There was no wind going on. And suddenly the cold whisper fell in his ear again - 'you are looking in the wrong room.' Sunil felt as if there was someone inside him. He hurriedly came out of the room. Yashwant followed.

The inspector now stood in the hallway. What was happening to him? Was he getting mad? He could not understand. Then his eyes fell on the wall. Was it a figure? He could see the shadow of a man falling on the wall. He turned to see, thinking it obviously being of Yashwant as there was no one else in the hallway. But was it really of Yashwant? Yashwant stood on his right and there was not enough light in the way so that a shadow so dark and clear as the one on the wall could be formed. Fear gripped Sunil as he tried to understand whose shadow it was when it suddenly disappeared. Sunil looked all around him. But there was no sign of the shadow anywhere. He perspired profusely. Yashwant understood something was wrong. Naturally he hadn't seen the shadow or perhaps the shadow hadn't made itself visible to him. The manager put his hand on the cop's shoulder and asked, "what happened, sir? You look terrible."

"A good friend," the whisper became prominent once again, "not really good."

Sunil was getting the matter a little now. Someone was trying to tell him something. He had to understand what. He saw the shadow again, and this time at the edge of the stairs. He decided to follow it, so he hurried, towards it. The shadow moved just as swiftly as any natural man would while getting down stairs, only difference was it moved through the walls. Sunil followed it. Yashwant followed Sunil.

Sunil did not stop until he stopped at the door of the basement. There were only two constables here who were about to leave the place. Seeing their senior, they saluted at once. “There is nothing here, sir,” one of them said. But Sunil did not pay any heed to them and went in, with Yashwant right at his heels. The basement was a large room with junk all around. Sunil gestured Yashwant to switch on the light. When it was done, he could see what lay in the room. Empty cartons filled most of the dirty place, old and broken wooden furniture, torn curtains, and many other things that lay everywhere. Cobwebs filled every corner of the hall. He coughed twice due to the dirt in the air while passing among some old cardboard boxes. But what was he looking at, he could not decide. The shadow was nowhere to be seen now. He looked all around but there was nothing to be suspicious of.

All of a sudden the whispers came again. “Yes, right place, this is the right place...” It seemed as if more than one person whispered in his ear but he could not distinguish how many were they, and neither could he understand whether it was the voice of a male or a female. “Come here, come here...” the voices called him. Bewildered he looked all around, but once it seemed the voices came from one corner, then next moment it seemed they came from the other corner. And then he saw the shadow again. It was right on the wall in front of him just a few paces away. Sunil turned around once to make sure the shadow was not of Yashwant or any of the constables and it was the same ghostly apparition he had been following. The constables were outside the basement and Yashwant’s shadow fell on the other side. So, Sunil gathered courage and walked towards the ghostly shadow. The voices came along with. “Same place....

This is the place....yes".

Finally, Sunil reached the wall and touched it with his palm. The shadow wasn't moving. He touched where the shadow stood, staring at it, awestruck. Analyzing the wall from all points he was about to turn away from it when he gave one final try and knocked the wall. There was some sound. Sound like it was hollow from within. He knocked it again. Same echo. The cop understood that this part of the wall was very thin and it was possible there could be a small room behind it. He called the constables. Yashwant said looking at the constables coming, "what...what happened sir?"

"You will soon find out," said the inspector. When the constables came, he ordered them to brake the wall down. "No, no sir," said Yashwant, "you can't do this."

"Really?" asked Sunil, "and why can't I?"

The constables didn't want their senior to get angry and so they found some old metal tools and began their work. Yashwant said again, "sir, Mr. Raman is a very strict person. He will get really angry. Please try to understand. There is nothing behind it."

"Then you shouldn't have any problem if it brakes," said Sunil, "And as far as your boss is concerned, don't worry, I will handle him."

The weak wall soon gave in and broke into bricks. As Sunil had deducted, there was space behind it and was now visible. But along with the small room something else was also visible. Bones. Two skulls lay on the floor along with the bones, staring eerily at them. Tattered old clothes lay all around the small space. "Sir," one of the constables called. Sunil looked inside and said, "so, we really have a dead body in here, why Mr. Yashwant?" And he held Yashwant's collar. But Yashwant was ready. He had already taken up a log and hit with it on Sunil's forehead. Sunil shrieked with pain as the manager jerked himself from him. Everything went black in front of Sunil's eyes.

"Wake up.....wake up. It's time..."

Was he dreaming or was he hearing the whispers again? Sunil could not understand because when he came to and sat up, he found himself in a hospital room and with no one inside. Presently, one of the constables from the basement came in and saluted. Sunil looked enquiringly at him. The constable said, "Yashwant was trying to flee after hitting you, but we grabbed him. We locked him up after bringing you here. He was reluctant at first but when we showed him the stick, he began talking."

The story, as told by Yashwant went this way - There was no one called Mr. Raman in Kolkata. Yashwant himself was the owner of Johar. He had just made up a story of some Raman being the owner of the hotel and who was at present in Kolkata. And all this was just to hide the heinous crime he had committed nine years ago. He had bought the place along with the hotel before constructing Johar. But he hadn't paid the owner Santosh Lal all the money. Actually, he wasn't in the mood to. But Santosh Lal was a poor fellow and he couldn't fight with a big man like Yashwant. His hotel was demolished and Johar was constructed in its place. But until the hotel was constructed, Santosh Lal kept asking for the rest of the money. Now, Santosh Lal had a daughter and she was beautiful. Yashwant had seen her when he used to go to Santosh's house to make a deal for the place. Three days after the inauguration of Johar, he called Santosh for a party. He promised he would pay all his money. He invited him with his family. He knew Santosh had only his daughter for a family. Poor Santosh might have thought his daughter would feel good in a party. But was there really a party? Santosh could only realize it to be a trap when they the two were surrounded by three men and taken upstairs on the fourth floor, room no. 043. There, the old father was beaten thoroughly by the men while the daughter was ravished by Yashwant. After that the father and daughter, all injured, bloody and tired, were taken down by the lift, into the basement. There Yashwant had made the cabinet in the wall beforehand. The two were thrown inside it and the walled alive. They had died a suffocating and painful death.

Sunil's blood was boiling when the story finished. He went straight to the police station where Yashwant was locked. He told the constable to open the lock. Yashwant couldn't understand at first, but then, he had understood the facial expressions of the cop. He knew what was to happen next. And it happened alright, however much he pleaded. The rung fell on his body at all places and it fell continuously until it broke into two and Sunil began breathing exhaustedly. Yashwant cried and pleaded but Sunil did not stop.

Next day he was to be taken to the court but as he was brought out of the lock up, Yashwant clutched at his shirt and shrieked. He had a heart attack. He died on the spot.

Sunil knew Santosh Lal and his daughter were in search of rectitude and so they were causing all the mishaps in Johar. Finally they got justice and Yashwant too died a painful death. But stories say that even after six months of Yashwant's death the whispers haven't died yet. Still people can hear faint voices in the hallways and lift of Johar. The hotel is now run by its trust and the trustees deny any such event and say people make up stories. But Sunil wonders are they really stories? One year hasn't passed after the manager's death yet, is another death awaiting Johar? Sunil will be relieved only when the year passes and any mishappening does not occur.

****

CHAPTER IV

UDAY

Megha pushed the brake pedal and brought her car to a halt. She looked out of the window. The old building stood there. There was no one around. It was summer and vacations had started. The school looked forlorn and deserted. She had come to this school about two years ago to teach social studies. It was the only school in the small village of Chandan Nagar, and that too it could provide education only till tenth. After that the students had to go to the nearby cities to study further. Megha now walked through the gallery of the two-story building, remembering her days spent here. She could feel how the old guard would have rung the bell today with his skinny hands and how the children would have begun running crying ‘holiday, holiday’. She smiled. Basically, she had come for change of weather. Since the last two or three weeks now, she had been seeing bad dreams. She would see herself in a cage, shrieking for help, but no help would come. Finally, when she could handle it no more, she decided to change the place for a while, take a holiday and rest for some time. What better place could be than Chandan Nagar to spend a few days?

She walked further and came to the small assembly ground of the school. There was a hand-pump here. She pulled down the handle expecting water. Nothing. This was strange for her. Two years ago when she was here, there was always water here. I mean, this is a school, she thought to herself, they have to maintain things. May be there might have been some problem. Another strange thing that caught her attention was that the guard was not there. The guard usually did not leave school until evening. And the holidays might have started only a day or two ago. He had to come here at least a week more according to the rules. Or had the rules also changed? Thinking he might have gone on some errand, she shrugged the issue off and walked further. Behind the school was a small ground where the children could play during recess. She did not go there. Then she decided to go and meet the people of the town. A few, whom she had known then. Like the principal, though she wasn't sure whether the principal then was still on job or retired and then there was 'Masterji'. 'Masterji's' bright son Uday. He was in class four then. She had to meet them.

She began walking faster when suddenly there was a banging from one of the doors. She stopped and turned. Right there from one of the classroom doors the banging came again. She was amazed and a little confused. Who could bang on a seemingly empty school door? Or was there really someone? Though she saw that there was no lock on the door. It was just shut. Naughty kids, she said to herself and opened the door. She was stunned to see Uday standing. He looked really bad. He was wearing his school clothes that were dirty and his hair was unkempt. His face had dirt all over like he had been playing in mud. His eyes were sullen and he looked as if he was sick. "Uday," Megha's voice came out but it was broken, "how come you are here?"

Uday blinked his eyes and looked at the woman carefully. Then said, "Megha ma'am, you came." And he wrapped his hands around her as if he had seen her after years, which was of course true. Megha ran her fingers through his hair and said, "look, what have you done to yourself. Come, I will take you home." Then touching his forehead she said, "my God, you are burning with fever."

Uday smiled, "now you have come ma'am, now everything will be alright." Megha could not draw the meaning of the mysterious words the boy said. She made him sit in the back seat of the car and she herself sat in the front. Then

she began driving. Memories came by and by as she drove slowly.

He always proved his name - Uday. He was very intelligent. At standard four he would be found doing class five math. Teachers were highly impressed by him. He was everyone's favorite. But everyone has some merits as well as demerits. Uday was a nonchallant kind of a fellow who talked less and spent most of the time with himself. He did not care for what he dressed or whether his hair was straight or not, he just liked being among the trees and in dirt. And he had very little friends too. While the other kids of the school would go about playing cricket or football, Uday would be found at the river bank catching fish or a frog or swinging on one of the branches of the great banyan tree by the pond, that was considered to be the humble abode of the witch by the town's wiser people. But everyone cannot be the same as others.

Uday's father Mahesh Chowdhary was a teacher himself and a very respectable man of the town. Of course, his workplace was a school in a village that was about 10 kilometers from the town. But at Chandan Nagar too everyone called him 'Masterji' and took any help or tuitions that he gave readily. But he used to worry about Uday. Yes, Uday was a bright student, talented and 'Masterji' was very proud about it but the way the boy showed his behavior gave him great disappointment. Any father would want his child to go about like other children, play cricket in the sun, whine at study time, fight, cry, run around. But Uday was the perfect son. Neither he liked playing cricket, nor did he whine at study time. As if he was ever ready to study and ever ready to play beside the river. Mahesh would say, "don't know what will happen of this kid." Others would say it was good he listened to his parents and his never fighting with her younger sister was awesome but 'Masterji' was doubtful about that too. Sometimes he would say to his wife - "I want him to do some mischief, anything. But this boy is so very perfect." "Like Lord Shri Ramchandra," his wife would say. Although his daughter was just the opposite. Like, playing whole day under the sun, always involved in some mischief or the other, fighting, pushing, crying, running, just like any other kid. "Everything will be alright," the mother would say peacefully. Mahesh would sigh and agree.

And then Megha came to the town. She was twenty-six then and beautiful. Big black eyes, long black hair, a nice little smile, and a walk that the town folk felt would fail any model. She was very happy with her new job.

Diamonds shine even in darkest places. She came to know about Uday very soon and she was too highly impressed by his talents. “Very good, Uday,” she would say whenever he answered a question and he would smile shyly and sit down. Any other subject would be completed or not, but the social studies homework was never left undone.

Megha was there only for six months as her marriage had been fixed and she had to leave. Though Uday had been very disappointed by the news. But she had promised him that she would come back one day, just to meet him. She had promised also to bring many gifts too for him. Now, Megha gave a quick glance on the back seat and decided she would give the gifts to Uday at his home itself. The house of ‘Masterji’ was not very far from the school. A straight dirt road, banked by mud houses and after crossing the temple that was in the middle of the village, ‘Masterji’s’ house was just round the corner. A group of children ran behind the car, laughing and giggling. Suddenly Uday shouted, “stop the car, ma’am. I will get down here.”

“But why, you have fever, you must go home,” said Megha sternly.

“No,” said Uday, “see, the village doctor’s house is nearby. I will show him my wound. Or else father will scold me.”

Megha stopped the car and turned back, “wound.” Uday showed her his elbow that had a small wound and it was still red. She shook her head and said, “since when did you come to do such mischiefs? And how did you get trapped in the room, tell me?”

Uday smiled and opened the door saying, “it’s a long story” and ran outside. Megha stared at him for a moment and drove again. She stopped only at Uday’s house then.

Masterji was very happy to see her. She was humbly welcomed, made to

sit and given water. But then she began about Uday and both his parents’ faces fell. She said, “this Uday I tell you, sir. He has grown so mischievous from before? I can’t even imagine him getting fried in the sun with wounds and all...” but then she saw the fallen faces of the parents and fell silent herself. "What happened?" She asked after a second.

"Which Uday are you talking about?" asked Masterji to her great astonishment.

"Your son, Uday, sir," she said.

"Come with me, child," said Masterji seeing his wife to start sobbing. Megha followed him in an inner room with great confusion on her face. Mahesh stopped before the wall and pointed to a portrait hanging on it that had flowers around it. It was Uday's picture. Megha's mouth dropped open. "Our son, Uday," said Mahesh, "is no more. He died two years ago."

Megha sat down on the cot holding her head. "No, no, no," she said again and again, "this can't be possible. No, not possible." Then she looked up at Mahesh and said, "you are mistaken, sir."

Mahesh looked at her blankly. "I took his dead body in these old hands of mine, child. Any father's last wish is that his son puts fire to his dead body, but I had to put fire on my own son's." His voice gave way. His daughter brought him a glass of water from inside. She went in when she saw Megha getting uneasy and brought her another glass of water. Megha emptied it in one go.

There was a pause for a few moments, then Megha said, "then who was it whom I brought out from the closed room at the school and dropped him at the doctor's house? I talked so much with him..."

"It certainly was some other boy," said Mahesh, "I am sorry, but you have been badly mistaken."

"It could be Uday bhaiya's spirit," said Mahesh's daughter suddenly. She

was standing nervously by the door.

"Roshni, I have told you several times not to talk nonsense," began Mahesh harshly when Megha smiled and gestured her to come to her. The little girl walked up to her. Mahesh fell silent. "In which class do you study Roshni?" she asked making her sit on her lap.

"Four," Roshni said.

"And why do you believe it was your brother's...." the rest she could not say.

"We hear strange noises every now and then in the school. Laughing, chattering, footsteps, so loud, everyone believes it's a ghost. And I believe it is bhaiya."

"Always talking nonsense, the elder students have taught her all this. Go in, Roshni," said Mahesh sternly. Roshni scurried back inside.

"I believe her," said Megha firmly, "because the boy I was with in the car was not some other boy. It was Uday."

This time, Mahesh sat down on the cot holding his head.

After lunch Megha talked to Roshni for a little while. She asked her whether she herself had felt the strange sounds she had mentioned earlier. "Not the walking or chattering and laughing, but yes," she said, "one day while I was packing my bag for coming back home and all others had left, I heard a loud banging on the door that came from just beside my class. I thought someone was trapped. I ran to help him and opened the door that was shut. But inside the classroom, there was no one." And Roshni fell extremely nervous while saying this. "The other students say they have experienced it too. They say, they have heard someone laughing in empty classrooms, someone running...." Megha could only give the little girl a tight hug when her voice broke off.

When the heat resided a little towards beginning of dusk, Mahesh took Megha to show his fields - a simple excuse to talk something serious, Megha thought. But Mahesh was hesitant about something, and as soon as she observed this, she started herself. "So, when did this happen?" she asked.

"What?" Mahesh asked as if started.

"Uday's death, when did he...?"

"The last day of your working," came the reply, "the same evening you left for your marriage."

Past memories began flashing in front of Megha's eyes. Uday had been very upset at the news of her marriage and the knowledge that she would go away forever was rending his heart. May be due to this he had fallen ill. He hadn't come to school for the last two days. But on the last day of her working, he had shown up. Though he was weak and still on medicines, he argued he had to come because his favorite teacher was leaving that day. He had to meet her. So Megha had told him to go to the last bench of the class and take rest. He had done as told. And when classes were over, she had forgotten all about her student....

Megha turned to Mahesh. She said, "what had happened that day?"

Mahesh gave out a heavy sigh and said, "when he didn't return even when it got dark, we began to worry. But still I thought he was only a kid, might have gone to someone's house or might be playing. When it struck nine in the clock I began to worry too. I asked all relatives and his friends, he was with no one. Finally, I went to the school to take a look. I had taken the guard along. He continuously argued he had locked the doors himself and there was no one in the class. How wrong he was."

"Was Uday....?"

Mahesh nodded, "he was still in the class, asleep. Very ill. When the guard opened the door, we found him asleep on the floor beside the blackboard. His clothes were dirty, he was all sweaty and his body was literally burning. Oh, how many times he might have pounded on the door? I took him straight to the

doctor. But...."

"But, what sir..?" Megha's voice cracked.

"Who has been able to fight fate? We couldn't save him. He died that day."

Megha sat down on the floor. It was all her fault. She had told him to take rest in the last bench. She had forgotten about him when school was over. It was because of her that the little boy had slept till the last and the guard had locked the door. Because of her he had been trapped there. Because of her, he died...... tears rolled down her cheeks and she couldn't stop herself. She began crying like a small kid. Mahesh was surprised. He tried to console her but she wouldn't stop. She told him her part of the story. Mahesh understood, kept silent and decided to leave her alone for the moment.

"It was around after a month or so that the children began complaining that the water from the hand pump was not coming," said Mahesh. It was night time and dinner had been served. Megha, Mahesh and Roshni sat around the table. "And soon after that, they said they were hearing banging and laughing and all that nonsense. I didn't believe a word of it. I thought the children were playing pranks."

"But they are true," said Roshni.

"Roshni, keep quiet and eat your food," scolded her mother, "how many times I must tell you that you should not talk when elders are talking?" Roshni fell silent.

"I am leaving tomorrow morning," said Megha, chewing.

Mahesh swallowed and said, "do whatever's right." Maybe there was a feeling somewhere in his heart that this woman was somehow responsible for the boy's demise. If she had remembered... perhaps.... Megha understood this fact, all the more reason that she would flee any moment now.

***

"I didn't even look at the school when I was driving back," said Megha. She was in Kolkata where she had been married, and now she sat in front of a counselor. She had decided to come to see this woman when after returning from the village she had not been able to sleep three nights in a row. Ravi, her husband, was worried and told her to take help. So now she sat before this middle-aged counselor called Mrs. Ganguly and told her the whole story of Uday.

"You really believe the boy you had brought out of the class was Uday?" the woman asked adjusting her round glasses.

"What's not to believe, Mrs. Ganguly? He was Uday.

Alright?" said Megha irritated.

"Okay, okay," said the old woman. Then she looked through her notes again and said after a moment, "you don't need medicines, my child. Your problem is somewhat different."

"What is it?"

"You may now be believing that this is a paranormal problem?" Mrs. Ganguly asked smiling.

"Ye...yes," said Megha as if she didn't want to say the word. Rather she didn't want to believe what was happening was true. No common man can believe.

"It's okay, my child," said Mrs. Ganguly, "the only problem was in the school and you have unknowingly finished it."

"But... but, I don't understand..."

"I will explain it to you," said the old woman, "look, you said you had forgotten about the boy who was left asleep and locked up. When he woke he found himself trapped. Like anyone, he also became afraid and he might have begun thrashing at the door like mad. But there was no use. Now, he slept off then and there and didn't even realize that he had been rescued by his father and taken to the doctor, where eventually he died."

There was a little pause. Mrs. Ganguly went up to the window with her coffee mug. "Now, comes the real part," she said, "Uday's soul had been trapped in the classroom itself. And it thought that no one has rescued him yet, without his knowledge that he is dead."

Megha's mouth dropped open. Was this really possible? But then she recalled her story and said to herself it could very much be possible. Mrs. Ganguly continued, "that's why the children were hearing banging on the doors, laughter, and all sorts of noises. Uday's soul was trying to make contact because he felt..."

"That he was trapped and somebody would rescue him," completed Megha.

"And you, my child, did just that," said the old woman smiling, "you freed his soul."

Now, Megha understood what Uday had meant by his mysterious words when he had said - 'now you have come, now everything will be alright.' Now she understood the whole matter. This meant all the noises of the school would have stopped. Megha thanked Mrs. Ganguly and began going when the old woman said again, "and if you go back to the village, check the water too, from the hand-pump." Megha thanked her and left.

***

Megha stood in front of the school. The kids declared that they had not been hearing any noises lately. Since it were the holidays, they didn't come to the school though, but surely they came to the ground to play and from there too, noises could easily be heard. All was now calm and quiet like before. The hand-pump was running water again. And that was enough proof for Megha that everything was alright again. Her dreams didn't come anymore. She could sleep peacefully now.

****

CHAPTER V

THE DAY IS COMING

The old man looked as if he was of hundred. Completely bald, long white beard that reached the chest, eyes that seemed like they would fall out of their places any moment, and it looked like not a single muscle was left in his body. Sometimes he shivered so much like a thin leaf in a hurricane that it seemed his body would disintegrate into parts. All that covered his body was a white banyan and a blue lungi and all he had as a legacy was a thin rag like blanket over which he used to lie down and a mosquito net that was tattered from many places.

Arun passed him every day, noticed him every day, but never said anything. His school timing didn't allow him to, not that he was all eager to. He would go over this path, i.e. through the park everyday on his bicycle at nine in the morning. This path had been shown to him very generously by his friend Mahesh, as according to him not a single ray of the hot sun touched the place and Arun had observed that it was true, as being part of the park, the dusty path was banked by trees from both sides, plus he could reach school within ten minutes now. Another thing that interested him was the perpetually lingering cool breeze that freshened him up always. It was a dense growth of trees basically, the backside of the main park. But there were trees enough to give the feeling of a jungle and even a thin rivulet flowed through it too with a cement bridge over it. Arun had to cross it every day, and he fancied the area as a place in some kind of a horror story.

This place, i.e. this jungle was home to a few homeless, fateless citizens of the city. There was this pair the man of which would bath at the rivulet everyday and wear the only shirt and trousers he had adding them with leather shoes and start his day with a thela having various goods like biscuits, cigarettes, tobacco and gutkhas. There were three-four young lads that had no other work than to laugh and chat and listen songs from their mobile phones. Sometimes there would be one or two cyclists too, who on their way to work would very patiently wait for their other friends to come and join them. And there was this lean and thin old Muslim fellow who would shake like a leaf in a hurricane.

Arun noticed everyone, but this old man always caught his eye. Mornings and evenings, both times the old man lay there on his place - the clearing under the great peepal tree. Sometimes he would be found lying asleep under his tattered mosquito net. Then Arun would give a sad glance at the other fateless people of that place and think - 'these people also don't help him.' Then he would think- 'these people themselves don't have homes, how will they help others.' His class hours would be over by 3.30 and he would leave school as soon as possible. But when he passed over the bridge, his eyes would automatically fall on the old man who would still be there on his same old place. When he saw him, the old man too would stare at him with his big protruding eyes and Arun would quickly look other side. The old man seemed creepy to him.

***

That evening as Arun walked over the thin cement bridge with his cycle, his eyes automatically went over to the old man's place as usual. There under the mosquito net he sat, shaking as ever. Today Arun decided, he would talk to him. When he went nearer, he moved his eyebrows at the old man and said, "what's up?"

The old man said nothing, but just stared at him with his hollow eyes. Arun felt quite awkward - both at his gesture as well as the old man's reaction - although there was no reaction at all. He shrugged and walked on. Suddenly there was a shaky voice behind him - "what's the time, child?" Arun turned to see the old man pointing with a long bony finger over his other wrist - imitating for a watch. Arun looked at his watch and said, "oh, it's 3.45."

"Ah, been quite some time," said the old man, "and she is still not here."

Arun wasn't the one to pry over other's matters and so just to keep up his principal, he didn't reply anything to the old man's words, though at this time he felt the greatest urge to ask who was he talking about. He just walked on.

Next day, as Arun passed the old man, he asked himself, “and, going to school?”

Arun smiled and said, “yes.” That was a small talk between the two and Arun didn’t say any further, just walked on.

That afternoon while returning, Arun decided to take something for the old man, just out of the sake of their small talking. He bought a packet of biscuits at the school canteen. When he reached the park, he handed it over to his old friend. As was obvious, the recipient was hesitant. “Oh, please take it,” said Arun, “it’s just....a just...” He couldn’t find the right words. He was always at a lack for words at moments of these kind. But to his relief the old man took the biscuits from him and he just put up his shaky palm for blessings. Arun smiled and walked away, but after going a few steps, he stopped and hid behind a tree to see what was being done to his biscuits. He saw the old man tear the pack with some difficulty and put a biscuit in his mouth. Arun smiled and headed for home.

The biscuits became a link - a starting point for the friendship between the two. Whenever Arun passed him, the old man would ask general questions - like ‘going to school’ or ‘how are you’ or ‘what time was it’ and this and that. Sometimes Arun began the talking and sometimes the old Muslim. One day, while returning in the evening, Arun sat and talked to the old man for some time. There was nothing else to do at home, there were no tuitions today. So he decided some talk with his old pal would do no harm. They talked for around half an hour. Both of them shared about their lives and all. Arun said how he had to take up science due to his father’s pressure against his own will. He told him about his dream, that he wanted to become an archeologist and his father wanted him to become an engineer.

The old man shared about his life as well. His name was Rahman, and he was alone. He had no one else - no family and no relatives. Yes, he had a family once, when he was young. “I was around 18 or 19 then,” he said remembering, “we were in Dilli then”. His father was a *vaidya*. He used to cure people with his knowledge of rare roots and leaves. He tried passing his legacy to his children also. Rahman's mother helped his father in the work. Life was happy, but then the monster came. They all lost their lives during the 1947 separation when he along with his family was trying to move to Pakistan. As he told his story Arun couldn't understand whether the old man's eyes were filled with woe, or anger. Death and destruction lingered all around. His family fell prey to the monstrous affair as well. Rahman was the last survivor of his family. He too would have been dead, thanks to the stranger who pulled him just in time into his house and saved him. His stalkers had not seen him and went to another lane in search of him. He had cried so much at his loss. He cursed himself for being alive and to Allah to let him live. His savior consoled him, told him that God has given him life, he should put it to some use. That there might be some motive behind it.

He understood this and when the conditions became a little stable, he thanked his host and left his house. Rahman left the city altogether and found a village where he could live peacefully. But there was no peace in his mind. All the time he would think about his family. Their dead faces roamed in front of his eyes all the time. He left that place as well.

There was a mosque just outside the village. He went there before leaving. There he wept again. Rahman remembered, there was no one there then. Then it happened. As he knelt and bowed down his head, he suddenly felt warmth upon himself. It was evening and it was a little cold outside, so how could he feel warmth inside? He looked all around. There was no one and nothing unusual that could make him feel like that. Was it then the grace of God? He was not sure. Whatever it was, he had knowledge of something now. He knew his fate and he thanked Allah for it.

"What was it? What did you learn?" asked Arun. Rahman continued, "it was something with which I could help people." Actually, he had gained knowledge of herbs. The same knowledge that his father had and which he was learning from him before the cursed events and which could never be completed. Knowledge of rare roots and leaves which could cure diseases. All of a sudden, he knew them now. He went to the next village where he found a small hut just outside it. There he began practicing his knowledge. People of that village soon learnt about this new doctor and he was famous within a month. His pastes were working. He was doing miracles. But he would not charge much from the poor people. The divine warmth had given him wisdom as well. He soon left that village as well because for anything he was, he was a human and he was young, sometimes the confusion, the hatred, the sadness of his past experiences came to him like a ghost. He could not attain peace of mind then. So, he never remained at one place. He moved from village to village, helping people, saving lives. And finally, after so many years he came to this place. This peepal tree gave him quite some peace to his mind. But now he was old, and he couldn't help people with his great knowledge. His house was the base of the peepal tree and his fooding came with great difficulty. Generally, the hawkers that put up for the night in the area gave him food, but sometimes he couldn't get anything. Arun felt really sorry for him. Rahman said he was just waiting when Lord would call him and he would go. Now, he just wanted to count his last breathes. Arun now got the urge to ask about that day when he had told *it was time but she had still not come*. He asked, "So that day you said it's six and she is still not here. Were you waiting for someone?"

Rahman was silent for a few moments. Then as if remembering, he said, "oh, that day. It was nothing."

Arun didn't ask again and began looking the other side. He stared at the trees and thought different things at the same time. How long would it take to reach the main park from here? May be the old man has completely forgotten about that day? Or is he trying to hide something? Why should I care? Then Rahman said, "you will find this funny, but I was waiting for death that day."

Arun looked at him with amazement. Then he smiled and said, "that is a poor joke, uncle."

Rahman didn't smile. Instead he stared at Arun with his protruding eyes and said, "I told you, you would find it funny."

At once the environment grew uneasy for Arun. He got up and said, "I will leave now, I think. It's getting dark." And he walked as fast as his feet could

take him.

Arun had heard stories where old people talk about their final moments. His own grandfather had told him once, "I am just waiting for my death now, child, there's nothing that I want now." But this Rahman - he was different. He said he was actually waiting for death that day. And he wasn't joking. He felt something in his gut. What a strange fellow - this Rahman.

***

Days passed and Arun got busier. Too much work load made him forget all other things. His exams were getting closer and the school was giving extra classes for the syllabus to finish. Also, the tuitions that he was taking would become another headache. He would just stop going to the tuitions one day, he had decided. During this, he didn't get much chance to see Rahman. It wasn't that he had got afraid of the old man's ridiculous talk, (well, perhaps he had got a small shock) he just didn't feel like talking. Moreover there would be two to three extra classes in a single day sometimes and it would get dark when he returned. Rahman would be fast asleep by then.

And then, finally he decided enough was enough. He quit going to the tuitions. Extra classes at school were too much to handle, lest talking about private coaching. He would study on his own. He would make it. He felt quite light now. As if, he had been relieved of a headache. While returning home one day, he decided to talk to Rahman. He reached up to his perch and said, "uncle?"

Rahman lay on his perch with eyes closed. He heard the well-known

voice and sat up shaking. "Oh, Arun," he said, "seen you after a long time."

Arun had brought patties for the old man. He handed it to him and said, "sorry, couldn't meet you. Too much work load."

"I understand," he said, and taking the patties added, "you don't have to do so much."

"Oh, it's nothing," said Arun, "moreover, I have left my tuition classes."

"Oh, why?"

"Just didn't feel like it," he replied, "I will study on my own. My father wants me to become an engineer. But I will have to pass the exams first. I will do it, let's see what happens. Tuitions are not always necessary to understand everything. May be...may be I will tell dad after the results come, that I want to become an archeologist and not an engineer."

Rahman nodded and took a bite of his patties. "No one knows what the future contains," said he, "good thing, at least you are building your future yourself. Your father will understand, I am sure."

"We all build our futures ourselves, uncle," Arun said.

There was a moments' pause. Suddenly Rahman said, "well, the day is coming now. So, I suppose this will be the end of our friendship."

"What day is coming?" asked Arun innocently, "are you going somewhere?"

The old man nodded, "very far. Day after tomorrow. These are my last two days here."

Arun sat down on the ragged cloth and began staring at the trees. A light breeze swayed the thin branches to and fro. Perhaps he was a little sad at the old man's words. But he never showed his feelings to anyone. "So where are you going?" he asked after some pause.

"Don't know, let's see," Rahman said.

"Why are you going, anyway? I know you have travelled all your life, but please give some rest to yourself."

"Everyone has to go one day. No one can live forever in one place. Anyway, this will be my last journey."

Again, the strange ridiculous talk. Why does he have to talk like this? Wandered Arun. Then he got down ready to go. "Arun," said Rahman holding his hand suddenly, "you have been very nice to me. You are a kind fellow. Thank you."

Once again Arun couldn't decide why was his friend talking like this. May be this was his way of saying good-bye. He said, "I will come to see you day after tomorrow. What time will you go?"

"Now, I am not sure. Let's see," said Rahman brooding, "you come by noon, yes."

Arun said goodbye and left.

***

His eyes opened late that morning. When Arun looked in his cell phone, it was already 10. "My God," he murmured, "Rahman's going to leave today and I am late." He freshened up as fast as he could, cursing himself for watching movies the whole of the previous night. What could he do? He had been studying quite hard since the last few days. One break was justifiable. He rode his cycle as fast as he could to reach the peepal tree. But when he reached the place, he was confused to see a crowd gathered around the place where Rahman slept. He increased his footwork and reached the crowd. Cutting through the people, he found Rahman lying in his bed, eyes closed. Two men were untying the mosquito net while a photographer from some local newspaper took photos of the old man. Flies flew on Rahman's peaceful face. He was dead.

People were whispering among themselves about him. "How did he die?" one asked.

"Don't know," said another, "but he was too old. How many days would he live? God called the poor man quite late."

Another man said, "I pass this way every day. Always found him sitting. But today he lay asleep. I knew something was wrong."

Arun came out of the crowd and sat on his bicycle, his legs on the ground to balance. He was totally confused. Rahman was going somewhere today. He was leaving the place. How could this happen? And then it got to him. He was talking about this only. He was talking about his death. That's why he talked so weirdly. He had told Arun about his waiting for death one day and he hadn't believed him. So, he never told him directly the day before. But he gave him hints continuously. "The day is coming, this is the end of our friendship." "No one lives in a place forever." The words of Rahman rang again and again in his head. He looked at the trees in the distance. The wind swayed their thin branches. A tear came at the corner of his eye. He rubbed it off. So incredible, a man knowing the day of his death. Only if everyone knew about the future, what would it be like? Arun imagined, but then, there would be no fun in life. He stayed there for some time, then walked off as the crowd decided to take the body to the hospital. This old man would remain in his thoughts forever. May be now he had found the peace he was in search for.

****

CHAPTER VI

SHE IS A WITCH

I stared at the paper that my clumsy fingers held and read the things written on it. I had no idea what they meant. Not the least idea. God! Mom would kill me if I got less than ten in this test. This was the third class test of our standard twelfth term at The Ayappa Public and I had got less than ten in both the earlier tests. But what could I do? Chemistry was a thing that went above my head...always. Same was the condition with my partner, Ravi, too. But his condition, seemed to me at least, was better. Because he was smiling. Perhaps he was thinking something? I would ask him later about it but for now the questions were giving me a headache. And why wouldn't they? All of them were numericals. I could answer theoretical questions a little, but numericals? They were a curse for me. Moreover, Ravi's smile was increasing my headache. Why the hell was he smiling? I decided I would ask when the class was over. For now, I decided to write something that would even seem a little like an answer.

Ravi and I were friends from, I think class two or three, and were best friends. We both were average students when it came to studies, but when it came to chemistry, we both were hopeless. Our mothers would blame us for this. My mother would say Ravi had ruined me and his mother would say I had ruined Ravi. And we were unable to explain them that we were spoiled brats. Yes, our fathers knew this fact alright. My father would not blame Ravi for my poorness in studies but he would say, "always playing and watching tv. I will throw away the television one day. Don't have any other work to do. Only watching tv. Why don't you study a little?" Ravi's father too blamed the television for his little brain. Whatever it was, we were same in many respects and we were fast friends.

The bell rang and the teacher collected all the papers. She glanced at me once while taking my answer sheet and sighed. She knew we were hopeless. She took Ravi's paper too and left. I asked him, "why were you smiling?"

"What? Who? When?" asked Ravi, as if started.

"During the test, you ass," I said, irritated, "I saw you smiling. Why?"

"Ah...that?" he said. And I saw he was blushing. He said, "when a hot teacher is taking your exam, why care for the dumb test? I was staring at her all the time."

"Her face? Or her figure?" I asked mocking him. I was really worried about the test. Mom had given me deadline. I knew her *belan* would be ready when the result of the test would be handed to us.

"What do you think?" said Ravi and winked. He was right. I hadn't seen a more beautiful woman in my life before. The new chemistry teacher in school was just that. Her age could not have been beyond twenty-five, and she always wore dark colored kurtis with really dark colored jeans. Her kurtis would be mostly blue or green and jeans, that as Ravi said, "see, the fitting, man" would be dark blue or black. She looked astonishing in them as she was fair-skinned herself. She made her back level hair into a pony and wore glasses. She had come to this school only a month ago and every boy in school had gone 'wow' at her. Only then we had realized she had come in replacement of our earlier and much older chemistry teacher Miss Breganza, who had gone somewhere. Good for us, I had thought, she always took the toughest exams ever. But this test told me that our new teacher Miss Shreya Mallick was just a younger version of Miss Breganza. Not that I didn't enjoy looking at her 34-28-36 figure but I always went for the face first and yes, Shreya Mallick was beautiful. No one could deny that. It felt like the deer like eyes, and the long nose and those lips fit perfectly in the round face. Yes, she was a 'wow'.

But the test result was even more important for me than going wow on the teacher. Ravi was more of a free-living person. He did not like to take tensions. But when we both came out of the class for recess we found Miss Shreya standing by the door. "You two," she said, gesturing at us with her slender fingers. We stopped. "I know you both are little weak in chemistry," she said. Tell me something new? I thought. She stared at me for a moment, as if she had read my thoughts, then said again, "see, I will tell you only one thing. Study. Study hard. The exams are nearing and you have not been performing too well. Why don't you take private coaching for chemistry?"

"Coaching? And that too for chemistry?" Ravi said, controlling his laughter with great effort, "my father will kill me if I have to take tuitions for chemistry, ma'am."

I didn't say anything. Shreya Mallick looked at the two of us for some time, then said, "okay, do it like this. Study a little then come to me to clear your doubts. Anytime. After classes, during recess, you can come to me even at my home. You know the address, right? Then I can even teach you something."

I remained silent. But Ravi spoke, "ma'am, we can come to your house."

"That's great," she said, "see, you both are intelligent kids, I know. You just need to focus. Okay? Then drop by in the evening." Saying so, she left. We watched her go. And when she had turned round the corner I grabbed Ravi's collar. "Ma'am, we can come to your house," I mocked him, "what the hell were you thinking? Now we will go to her house? For tuitions?"

"What's the problem, man? Don't go nuts," said Ravi, smiling, "can't you see, the girl herself is inviting us."

"Yeah, as if you will go and she would be waiting there for you in her inners, why?" I said. I was always against tuitions. And I had taken care of it that I didn't have to take any yet. I was weak in studies, yes, but I managed to get satisfying marks in the exams. Just for the sake of avoiding tuitions, I used to study a little.

"Who knows, maybe she would do just that?" Ravi said. This didn't convince me. I kept staring at him. Then he kept his hand around my shoulder and said, "oh come on man, we are getting a chance to spend some time with a beautiful woman, let's go. At least for my sake. Let's give her chemistry a try."

But not today, I decided. Because the tests were going on and it was history the next day. I had to study. After that the tests would be over. And I promised Ravi, we would go tomorrow evening.

***

Next day, my history test went fine. I remembered the answers quiet well enough. As I told you, I was good in theory. After the test Ravi said, "I went there yesterday."

"What? You went there? Alone?" I asked completely surprised. Obviously, I knew what he was talking about.

"I didn't meet her," said Ravi, shaking his head, "I saw her house just.

From far. She lives near the forest. Nice area, that is."

The classes were over and we were on our way to Miss Shreya Mallick's house. Our school was in one corner of Sector- 5. You could say it was on the outskirts of the city because a forest started about 1 kilometer from it. It was not a big jungle, just a thick greenery beyond which slum dwellers lived. If Shreya had taken up her lodging in a house near the forest, it meant she could just walk to the school every day. But I hadn't heard of any houses anywhere near it. Though there was a building called Priya Apartments on the other side of the school, where mostly teachers of the schools lived with their families. But Shreya could not live there, because we were going in completely opposite direction.

I got my answer when we reached the place. It looked like some place in a fairy tale. A small cottage with asbestos roofing in a clearing with trees all around. The small yard had been converted to a beautiful garden. It was not that big hungry wild animals dwelt in the forest, as I mentioned earlier it was a small grove with so many trees, it almost seemed like a forest. But there were surely smaller animals present like rabbits, moles and snakes and they could easily come to this part of their habitat. Shreya Mallick was watering the plants. A long pipe went from the garden right into her house. She saw us coming and kept the pipe down. She was wearing a black pajama and a red top. 'She is really hot, man,' whispered Ravi. We parked our cycles outside the wooden fence and opened the gate. She gestured us to follow and entered the house.

"I didn't know there was a cottage here, near the forest?" I said.

"Even I didn't know. I was staying at a friend's room in market area. But she had to leave for her job. She is an air hostess. She had to leave the room too because the room owner wanted the room for some function. Before she went she told me about this cottage here and I came to find out. The dealer said he would give the whole house to me on rent. And what's more, the rent is quite low and the school is only at a walking distance. What more could I want?" She made us sit on chairs and gave a bottle of water. "So, are you ready to study?" she asked. We nodded. She pulled the table nearer and opened the chemistry book. Then she asked for a note-book, she would need to write. Ravi excitedly gave her his copy and a pen too. She began.

She taught quite well, I thought and I told this to Ravi too, while returning. But he said, "who cares for studies man, I was just staring at her." I hit him lightly on his arm. I decided I would go every day. Perhaps chemistry had some sense in it too.

That day I had a headache at night. I had to take medicine to get some

sleep. Never before had I ever got one. Perhaps the time I had spent outside today had completely drained me. So much study and no play makes me a dull boy. But one thing surprised me the next day. Ravi said, he had a headache too.

***

I had decided I would ask for Shreya's tuition fees. And I asked the next day. But she just stared at me with anger. Then, after a moment, she said, "the school pays me enough, okay? Did I ask for fees? You come here to clear your doubts. You have insulted my passion." I put my head down. I was filled with guilt.

Ravi took charge and said, "he meant ma'am, that like if we are taking tuitions here, like all teachers do, then there might be a fees as well."

"Like I said, the school pays me well," said our teacher, smiling, "and I want to extract the gems out of coal, okay? If I want anything I will certainly ask for it, okay? Now, did you learn the periodic table?"

That day, I enjoyed even more. But at night, the headache came to me again. I had to take the pills. I reckoned it was the extra time we were spending after school. Next day I told this to Ravi when he said he too had the headache again.

Now we were going almost every day to learn something from Shreya. She was a good teacher, teaching along with cracking silly jokes in between. A good company, I decided. But along with the studies, I had the headaches too. The day I went to her house, the same day, I had the headaches. And the day we didn't go, the headache didn't come. I read somewhere that about 70% of the energy from human body was spent when we worked with brains and not physically. That sorted out the matter for me for the time being. Same was going on with Ravi as well, and I told him this fact. That was enough to calm him down. But did I have any idea that the real problems were yet to come.

***

Shreya said she missed home-cooked food very much. Since she was not a good cook and that she was away from home, she missed the food cooked by her mother. I understood what she hinted by saying this. Next day I took my lunch and handed it over to Shreya. First, she hesitated, said I shouldn't have left the lunch for her. But when I urged she ate it. She praised my mother for cooking and said that the food reminded her of her home. But then she said I needn't have to bring my lunch given by mom for me. She said she would ask me to bring something when she felt like. So, when she asked she would like to have kheer, I readily got it made and took it for her. My mother was curious but as she said, "anything for studies, and anything for the teacher." And since the teacher wasn't taking any charges, making kheer was okay. Ravi too began bringing eatables. He wasn't going to be left behind. And this went on.

And then, that morning I fell ill. Seriously ill. I had high fever. The family doctor came, he checked, gave me different kinds of colourful tablets. I called Ravi to inform about my illness and that I would not be able to go to school today and to Miss Shreya's class too. But I was surprised when he said he was ill too. He was having high fever. The matter now was becoming strange. It was okay that we were working hard and so we got headaches. But every day and to both of us was certainly out of question, and now this fever. Mom was red with rage. She cursed. And she cursed everything - she cursed my school, she cursed Ravi too, she cursed Shreya Mallick. "That woman, why do you go to her," she said, "see what she has done."

"Mom, why are you acting like this?" I asked agitatedly.

"Why? Why does she call you after classes, and every day?" she was saying, "you get tired and see what has happened. You have fallen sick." Mom said she was a witch. Like any mother would say when her only child got sick in such conditions. "That witch, why doesn't she get lost somewhere," mom said throwing her hands in air. I sighed. I could not explain her. I myself was confused. I needed to talk to Ravi and to Miss Shreya.

Next day I got well and met Ravi at school. He looked fine. We discussed about the matter. "It's all fate, a matter of chance," he said in a poetic way, "we are best friends and we can fall ill together."

"You are hopeless," I said. He grinned.

That afternoon we went to Shreya's class. I told the matter to her, only the fever part. But she was very worried though but had no answer for it. It was that day when I came to know about her hobby too. I saw glass jars kept on wooden shelves on the wall and in them I saw animals - small ones - lizard, snake, there was even a bird, a canary in one of them, frogs, fish. They weren't there first, perhaps she had decided to keep where we could see them as well. They all were kept in some kind of liquid. "You have pets," I said.

"They are dead," she said, "the chemical keeps their bodies intact. You see, I found them dead. So, I decided why not to bisect them and see their internals? You see I like examining things. It's another of my favorite pastimes."

Weird pastimes! She showed us her microscope too. "You really have interesting hobbies, ma'am," Ravi said.

"I wanted to take up biology and study medical. But it didn't work

out," said she, "you see, we were not so financially strong that we could pay for it. So, I became teacher finally."

That day we left. And at night I fell sick again. Now I really got worried. You see, today we hadn't even studied in her class so that studying could be blamed for the fever. I understood something was going on. But what? I couldn't make out.

***

The exams were nearing and I had a lot to study. And for that I quit going to Miss Shreya's house often now. Though I had to persuade myself not to go there. You see, going continuously to her house and her technique of teaching had grown an attraction in me towards her. How little did I realize that going to her house would be so addictive. But I made myself remember what I really was. I was a free thinking, careless fellow and as soon as I realized that it was easier then not to go to her house anymore. Yes, I went there but only twice a week, just to clear my doubts. She asked one day at school about my absence. I told her I had to study. She said she was happy that she had been able to get me into studying.

Ravi on the other hand had grown his addiction even more. He went to her every day. And every day he grew more and more weak. And one day, just ten days before the half-yearly exams, I saw him as I had never seen him before. His eyes had sunk, wrinkles filled all his face and he had grown thinner - very thin. As if the entire life had been sucked from him. "What happened to you, pal?" I asked.

"Nothing," he smiled, "all study and no play has really made me a dull boy."

But it was not 'no play', I knew that. It was something else, something was going on with Ravi but I couldn't guess it. He said he had gone to the doctor and had been given medicines that he was taking every day since the last four days. But I could clearly see that they weren't working. "You go to Miss Shreya's class?" I asked. He said he was going there every day and he couldn't help going. She was teaching so well. Huh? That came as a surprise to me. The boy who was going to the teacher's house just to check her out was now going to her because he had to study. Even though it seemed absurd, I had the strongest feeling that going to Shreya's house was somehow responsible for my friend's health, that something was wrong with Shreya Mallick. I meant to find out what.

***

Next day was a Sunday. And on Monday, we had the practical exams. I decided to go to Shreya's house along with Ravi in the afternoon. The place was a little too quiet today. The birds didn't call. There was no breeze too. We went in. Our teacher was lighting a candle on a shelf. We stood at the door and watched her. She was wearing a black gown today. "I knew you would come," she said and turned, "come sit." Her voice seemed heavier and I couldn't believe she could put such kind of make-up. Her eyes were bordered deeply with kohl and she wore huge dangling ear rings. Her long hair fell loosely all over. She smiled. She had worn black lipstick too. "Sit," she said again.

We sat on the chairs. "Ravi's condition is getting worse," I said. Ravi was so weak, I doubt he had heard me. He had dozed off.

"You know why?" Shreya asked, going across the room and lighting another candle in a corner. I saw there were candles all around the room and she was lighting them one by one.

I was not getting the courage. The atmosphere was getting spookier. "May be...may be you could...tell," I heard myself stammer. She was having her back towards me but I was sure she was smiling.

"I have an answer though," she said. I didn't feel surprised though I was surprised at the thought that I had been expecting this answer only.

Suddenly the sound of the door close made me jump. There was no wind, and Shreya was standing at the other corner of the room. How could the door close on its own? Shreya stood up and said, "the water you were drinking from the bottle? When you came here and I offered you? Remember?" I could see the bottle on the table. We were drinking every day from it when we came here to study. "Well, now you understand why you fell sick and had the headaches?" She said, Yes, I understood quite well. That water was some kind of medicine or chemical or whatever to make us sick. And that was why Ravi had grown what he had grown into today. I shook him hard and he as if came back to life. "It can weaken anything," she said again.

"Who are you? What are you? Why are you doing this? What do you want from us?" I asked. Ravi didn't say anything. He was not in the condition to.

Shreya Mallick smiled. "You are quite a smart boy, why don't you figure for yourself? See, there's chemical in a bottle that can make you sick, there are candles all over, the door closed too."

It came to me suddenly. "You are a witch," As suddenly as the thought had come, as suddenly it came out my mouth. Shreya laughed.

"Wh...what?" I heard Ravi say, "this...this can't be..."

"And....and you want us for some sacrifice or something?" I said, though I hated to say it.

This made Shreya Mallik laugh even harder. I could see the sharp canines in her mouth. Her hair had grown longer. Her eyeballs had turned red. "You watch a lot of movies, I will give you that," she said in even hoarser voice than before.

"But there are good witches too, I have seen," I said, remembering from the various movies.

"White witches?" she said, "they are a bore. Making love potions, curing cancers, diseases. They like using their knowledge in other's interests. But we, the black witches...." She laughed again.

"What is...what is the...sacrifice for?" Ravi asked in a weak voice. I was feeling a little glad that he had realized the reality.

"You see, children, you think I am 24, you think I am young. But I have to work really hard to maintain my youth. Going to schools and luring boys with my beauty, then making them drink the liquid continuously is not always an easy job," she said, "you see you yourself quit coming to me. That's how it goes wrong."

"How...how old are you? How many schools have you visited?" came out from my mouth.

"How many boys have you killed?" Ravi asked.

Shreya laughed. "You guess," she said, then pointing to a pile of old newspapers she said, "you have a way to find out."

I ran to the pile and took a paper. The date on it read August 15, 1947. I looked at her in amazement. She said, "let's just say that I have seen the war for independence."

"You...you don't mean to say, you are older than that?" I said. She laughed.

"Run," said Ravi and I saw him standing at the door. I dashed for the door too. Ravi grabbed at the knob and tried to open it. But the door wouldn't

budge. I tried too. But failed. Shreya laughed again.

"You think I have done so much so that you can escape in the end?" she said, "you know how hard was it to find a house so isolated from the city? So that I could sacrifice young bloods like you."

"So, you don't have any friend in the city who went to air hosting?" I said.

"I make pretty good stories, don't I? Sometimes I think I can become a writer," she said.

Ravi began feeling uneasy. I helped him back on the chair. I sat too. "We are trapped," he said.

"We have exams tomorrow," I said.

"She will kill us," he said.

"We will miss the exams," I said.

"Are you out of your mind? First think of getting out alive," he said.

I took out my cell phone and said, "I am calling the police." But there was no signal. Ravi took out his phone too. No signals.

"No one's going to hear your shrieks," Shreya said, "Soon I will begin the necessary ritual and then...." She laughed. We had no way out. Now I understood the matter of those dead animals too. Witches work with them in making potions. Different potions to bring different results. Magic. Black magic. I shivered.

A few minutes later Shreya brought out three or four dried logs from a heap kept at the corner of the hall and lighted them too. Then she sat beside it, closed her eyes and began murmuring something. We just watched her. What else could we do? We were trapped. There was no way out. Moreover, how could you fight a witch who knew magic? "Get us out of here, or we are dead," Ravi said, "I don't want to die." I could see the fear in his face clearly. I myself was terrified.

But...but....then. It suddenly came to me. I moved forward and took the bottle of water on the table. I opened the lid and spilled the water on the fire. Shreya shrieked as the fire gave one final blast and died down. "No," she shrieked, "what have you done?"

"You said this liquid could weaken anything?" I said, "let's see what happens to you?" And I threw the water at her face. She shrieked again and tried to dodge herself as the water hit her. I kept sprinkling the liquid at her to keep her from getting to us. Naturally it was weakening her too. The candles died too and suddenly the door opened.

"Let's go," Ravi cried and I dashed as well, taking the bottle along with me. We closed the door behind us, locking the witch inside. She still was shrieking and trying to get the water away from her gown. We took our

bicycles and took off.

"Good thinking," said Ravi, later in the evening, "we were saved because you acted fast. But what now, do we tell our parents or the police? In case she attacks again?"

"They won't believe in the story of a witch. They will think we are making things up and wasting their time. Let's wait for a day and see what happens," I said. Ravi agreed.

Next day, Miss Shreya was absent. We had our lab exams. After that I asked another teacher about her. He said she had left. Shreya Mallick had resigned, by not coming here. Our principal had got a mail early in the morning from her stating that she had work at her village and had to go. She wasn't sure if she would return. This gave us great assurance though we didn't go to her house to see. When I returned home I told mom that the new teacher had left school. "That's good," she said.

I said again, "mom, you were right."

"About what?"

"She was a witch."

"What?"

"Nothing, I am hungry. Give me something to eat."

Later I checked my mail. There was one with no name. I read it and my eyes went wide. It was written - 'all my rituals went to waste. Luring you both, making you drink the water, taking edibles from you at intervals, then when you would be weak enough, calling you and slitting your throats. All was going fine but the day I ate the kheer made by your mother, I knew something was wrong. Even then I tried to lure you further. But then you quit coming to me and I didn't force you, I was dreading the result of the sweet dish. Yesterday you spilled the water that weakened me. But don't think that I am terrified of your sharp brain and fled. It's the kheer and all the cooked food from your mother that had weakened me since I had been having them. The water only ignited the flame. I am going, but I would tell you, keep a watch. There's a white witch at your home.'

***

CHAPTER VII

PILLS

"What the hell did he give me?" moaned Ritesh as his head reeked of pain. He looked at the leaf of tablets he had just thrown on the bed and cursed it. More than that, he cursed the doctor who had prescribed him the medicine. "It's a new medicine that has been given to the hospital for research as to how it works. Why don't you try it too?" Doctor Mitra had said cheerfully. Ritesh had slight fever yesterday. He had tried to sleep through it but when this morning he felt like all hell had broken loose on him, he decided to visit the health centre than to go to office. Dr. Mitra had become like a friend to him now, as since the past eight months or so he was showing himself to him, whatever happened. Dr. Mitra, general physician, knew the cure of almost everything. "Except aids and cancer," the doctor used to say, jokingly, "there's nothing impossible for me."

Now, Ritesh looked scornfully at the leaf of tablets. He took his mobile phone and dialed the doctor's number. "Yes, Ritesh, what is it?" asked the doctor on the other side.

"What did you give me?" asked Ritesh, "my head is paining like hell."

"And your fever? Is it gone or not?"

"The fever's gone," said Ritesh, realizing he was not feeling feverish all of a sudden. Feeling his forehead and neck he said, "now I have started a severe headache, doctor."

"Take some pain killer and try to sleep it off," the doctor's voice came, "it could be a minor side effect of the medicine."

Ritesh then cut the call. He had some painkiller in his drawer. He took it and threw himself on the bed. He slept. He dreamed.

He saw himself walking on a single lane that was flanked on his left by a mountain wall and on his left by a valley, the slope of which was very steep. It was evening and beside him was Riya - the girl whom he had loved for 5 years. She had loved him too.

Then some sourness had crept into their relationship. Right now, she wore a white frock the edge of which fluttered by the wind. Her long hair flew over her face and she very easily put the locks behind her ear by her index finger. They talked happily. He just stared at her face as she laughed. Suddenly there was the sound of honking and before the happy couple could understand anything, a truck came shakily towards them from the front. Its headlights shone with full blast and it seemed that the truck itself was in full speed. Ritesh understood that the truck's brakes had failed and he shrieked, "move Riya, it seems the truck's brakes have failed." He then pushed her aside towards the hilly wall and himself jumped towards her. But the truck was too near and poor Riya couldn't help herself. The truck hit her headlong. Suddenly, Ritesh sat up on his bed, shrieking. His whole body was filled with sweat and sleep was miles away from his eyes now. 'Only a dream,' he assured himself, 'nothing will happen to Riya. It was only a dream.'

It is but human nature that we try to know the whereabouts and health of our near and dear ones if we even dream about them. Ritesh did the same and he dialed Riya's number, though he knew she wouldn't talk to him. She was angry with him. And why wouldn't she? After you are in a relationship with someone for five long years and when your partner begins to think that you have become committed to her, you leave her and go to a bigger city to work and earn and that too without telling her, she wouldn't kiss you at least when you would next meet her. And here, the case was worse. Ritesh had called her three days after he had come to Ranchi and after patiently listening to all her abuses and swearing, had promised to return after a month. She had said she would not talk to him again and had cut the phone. Since then six months had passed and he had not gone home even for once and that too when it was only Bokaro that takes three hours by train or road. Though he had tried to call and assure Riya many times, but all she had said each time was that she hated him and she wouldn't talk to him anymore. Now, the bell rang and no one answered. He called again. Still no answer. He knew very well, she was there beside the phone and deliberately didn't pick it up. He called again. At last she picked it up, "hello, what is it?" her voice seemed full of anger and frustration.

"Look, please don't cut the call," he said, "I need to talk to you."

"Say fast," she said, "I don't have time."

"Yes, you have time, and you are saying this just because you don't want to talk to me."

"Well, you are smart," said the girl, "now that you have understood, so 'bye-bye'." She was about to cut the call when Ritesh persuaded to talk a little more. She sighed and said, "what is it, Ritesh? You know it's over between us."

"I am sorry for what I did, really," he said, "see, I just... you need to understand Riya, why I came to Ranchi. You see, we had graduated then and you know the economic crisis of my family was not leading me anywhere. I have to do something for my family, isn't it?"

"So, you came without even telling me," said Riya suddenly, "what did you think? Riya is a stupid girl, she will understand."

"Why, don't you come here? After all it's only Ranchi, you see," said Ritesh and at once felt very stupid.

"Going to Ranchi is not the question Ritesh," said Riya, "not telling is. And how can you say this so easily when you know my mother is ill and I and father both have to work in our hotel to buy mother's medicines?" She was almost screaming now, Ritesh could easily feel the moisture in her voice. She said, "now tell me, why have you called? Just to chat over this matter or what, because I have to go, I have work at the hotel."

"No, actually, I saw a bad dream about you and I just wanted to know that you were alright," said Ritesh.

Riya was silent for a few seconds. Perhaps she was amused at his innocence. So, he still has the softness to call and see if she was alright, even at a little bad thought or dream. But she said, "and why do you care, Mister Ritesh? Why do you care at all whether I live or die? Why does this even matter to you? Or is it that if you get the news of my illness, you will be very very happy?"

"Oh, don't talk foolish Riya," said Ritesh, a little annoyed, "I can't even think like that. Now, say how's everybody at home? How's uncle? How are you?"

"You don't have to think about me Ritesh. Whether I am alright, or I have met with an accident, this does not have to do anything with you. Whether a car has hit me or a truck, just don't call again." And the phone was cut.

Why did she say like that? Ritesh thought for a while. 'Met with an accident', 'hit by a truck'.... Ritesh decided to call her father and ask. He got the most shocking news of his life. Riya had really met with an accident. She was bringing rations for the hotel when a speeding truck had hit her from behind. She had a fractured leg and was admitted at the hospital.

***

Ritesh was bewildered. A dream coming true? Of course, he had heard incidents before where dreams had really become real. But that were not so intense. A road accident coming true, this was really something. Was it some kind of an omen? He thought, some sort of a foreboding? Finally, he gave up all thoughts and decided to pay the girl a visit. After all she was his girlfriend and he had come to Ranchi without even telling her. He owed her an apology. Moreover, he was not liking his job at the consultancy firm one bit. The money was also not good. Plus, he had one real grumpy boss who wanted his employees to work 24*7, even if there was not much work. It had been four months since Ritesh had begun working here and all his requests for an increment in his meagre salary had been dumped. He needed a holiday. And this was the best chance.

Ritesh thought and decided he would at least tell his parents that he was coming, then he would give the news at the office also. But just as he had picked up his phone again, it began ringing. It was his father. He answered and got another jump. His parents were coming to pay him a visit. And what more? They had even boarded the train and crossed two stations. His father said, "I wanted to give you a surprise, son, but your mother urged me to give you the news.

According to her, if we don't tell you, and if something happens to us on the way, you won't even be able to know. I thought she was right. So, we will reach Ranchi by another one and a half hour. Okay?"

Ritesh sat on his bed and put his head in his hands. It was not that he was not happy with the fact that his parents were coming, the main thing was, he had dreamt this one too. Only the night before, he had dreamed that he was in his home and he had paid his parents a surprise visit. Only it was a little different in the real world. Moreover, he was worried about Riya too. How was he going to meet her? He would have to receive his parents first. He finally decided that he would keep asking her father about her on the phone. And when his parents would decide to return home, he would join them. Next, he put his mind towards his dreams. What was happening to him? Was something really happening to him or was it just his whim? But two dreams coming true simultaneously? What about that? However much he thought, he couldn't track out anything. Finally, he let the thing go when his head began to ache. He decided it was nothing and he would only be serious about it when it happened the next time.

***

The room that Ritesh lived in, was a small place. What more would a bachelor need than a room, an attached bathroom and a kitchen and a few shelves to keep the regular things? But when his parents reached the room, they only said it was a good place for him. "It's little bit small for three people," he said.

"It would be better that you lived at home and did some job from there itself. Was it so much a bad place?" said his mother, "that you have to live in this junk?"

"Ah...Shanti," cut his father in between, "let the kid be. Don't start all over again."

"You people just get fresh, I will serve the food," Ritesh said and went into the kitchen, probably just to get away from the topic. After all he had fought with his parents to come here and get to his feet, and what had he achieved in the last seven months or so? A pity job in a pity consultancy, and that too he had got only because his boss had said - 'your communication skill is good.' Only after a few months of bone churning hard work, Ritesh had decided he would give up.

After lunch the old couple decided to rest for a while. Tired by the journey, they soon fell asleep. Ritesh came out of the room, on the road. He decided he would take a small holiday so he called his boss at the consultancy. But Raghubir Dasgupta was not at all in the mood to give his employees leave and he was really angry. He said, "listen Ritesh, I am running a consultancy here not so that anyone and everyone takes leave every now and then. You have been absent for two days Goddamnit without informing anyone and now you call me and instead of giving an apology, you ask for another ten days holiday? Am I looking like an ass to you or what? I pay you all Goddamnit...."

"Yeah, yeah, ten thousand is a lot of money," though Ritesh said this very softly as if to say just to himself, but the boss heard it and he boomed with rage, "what? What did you just say?"

This was enough for Ritesh. He said, "I said you *are* an ass and keep your job with yourself." Saying this he cut the call and thrust the phone in his pocket. He was angry but somehow somewhere deep inside he was feeling happy. He stopped by his regular shop, smoked a cigarette and then returned to his room.

***

One whole day passed since Ritesh returned with his parents back to Bokaro, after a day of staying in Ranchi, but still he didn't get the courage to go and see Riya. He hadn't informed her yet and neither her father. He would straightaway go and meet them at the hospital when her father brought lunch for her in the afternoon and even perhaps ask for her hand. May be then she will forgive him, but that would be later. Riya's father knew about their relationship and did not have any problems with it. On the other hand Ritesh's father had come to know of the affair accidentally when he saw the two in the City Park together. He used to go there for a walk as the park was very near to their flat. But he left the park and took another path for his walk since the day he saw his son with his girlfriend, fearful that he might see him again. But the same day, Ritesh had seen him as well and what's more? They had seen each other see each other as well. When both got home, neither of them talked to each other about the matter.

In the evening Ritesh called Dr. Mitra and told him about his return. The doctor only said, "it's your life Ritesh and you have to decide what you have to do." There was some more talk about the new medicines, although Ritesh did not tell about his dream coming true. He wanted to give himself time. After all he wasn't sure whether it was really happening or it was just a co-incidence. Then he said he would contact again if anything went wrong.

Next Ritesh called his friend Vikas Jha who worked as his colleague at the consultancy and told him about his quarrel with the boss. Vikas seemed a little disturbed by his voice but he said what Ritesh had done was right. Ritesh asked, "you don't sound well, Vikas, are you alright?" "Yes, yes, perfectly," said Vikas, "it's just this little fever I have got and nothing else. You don't have to worry." After that Vikas disconnected the call himself.

Since night had cast upon, Ritesh decided he would go to the hospital the next day. He still had his fever so he took one of the pills and slept. We see many things when we are asleep - sometimes our greatest wish is fulfilled, sometimes we ride on the weirdest fantasies, and sometimes we don't see anything at all. Ritesh saw too but it was something different. He saw his good friend Vikas Jha. He sat in his room, on his bed and smiled. Ritesh stood there in front of him watching him smile. But he could see something else as well. A pistol in his friend's hand. Suddenly Vikas unlocked the gun with a click and aimed it at his forehead. "No, Vikas," said Ritesh apprehensively, "you don't have to do this, wait. Nooo..." Before he could stop his friend, there was a loud bang in the air. Vikas had shot himself.

"No...." Ritesh sat on his bed horrified. It was just a dream, a really bad one. But two of his dreams had become real earlier. This fact terrified him more. He called Vikas again. First the bell rang for a long time but then someone picked it up and he hurriedly said, "Vikas, hi, it's Ritesh. How are you?"

"No, not at all. Your friend Vikas is not at all well," the person who spoke on the other side did not least bit seem like Vikas.

"What nonsense? Who are you?"

"I am Sub Inspector Sharma and for your kind information, sir, your good friend Vikas Jha has shot himself."

***

At first Ritesh could not believe what he had heard. He just kept the phone to his ear while the inspector poured down the cause of the suicide. According to the note found clutched in Vikas's hand, his wife had an affair going on and today afternoon he had caught her red-handed with her lover in his house. He had also mentioned that he had kicked both of them out of his house then but he could not bear his wife betraying him. He loved her so much. So, he was going forever from her life. Finishing the story the officer asked a few more questions like whether Ritesh knew where the woman could be found and etc, etc. he also said he might have to come to Ranchi for a questionnaire. Then the call was disconnected.

Ritesh was still awestruck. His third dream had come true as well. How could this even be possible? Vikas was sad when he was speaking with him, he had felt that. But electronics hide our emotions quite well and don't let the others see what really is going on. Ritesh threw the phone away. His phone was bringing all the bad news now-a-days. But what really was going on was confusing him beyond his wits. And Dr Mitra could possibly have an answer to this. He decided he would ask the doctor first thing in the morning.

Next morning Dr. Mitra received a call while he was doing breakfast of sandwiches and boiled eggs. "Oh, it's you, Ritesh," said the doctor on recognizing the voice as he hadn't given a glance on the screen as to who had called.

"I have a problem, doctor," said Ritesh.

"Yes, what is it?"

Ritesh told the doctor all that had happened in the last three to four days.

Then said, "what do you think?"

"Yes, it seems quite strange," said the doctor, "dreams coming real. This is really fascinating. But I don't think..." The doctor tried to say that it might be just co-incidence but Ritesh said in between, "look doc, I know what a co-incidence is. This has gone far beyond co-incidence." The doctor sighed and there was silence for a few moments. Then he said, "look, Ritesh, I don't think the medicines have anything to do with your dreams. Medicines cannot do that. It's totally absurd."

"Then what is it?" asked Ritesh, a little rudeness creeping in his tone, "you tell me doc, what is it? I will go mad if this carries on."

Dr. Mitra assured Ritesh that everything was normal and that he was overreacting. Now that he had gone home, everything would get back to normal. There was nothing to worry about. He also assured him that he would try to find out about his dreams just for Ritesh's sake. But all this assurance got Ritesh nowhere. He remained worried.

Ritesh's fear was not without reason. First he was thinking his dreams were just forebodings - some sort of omens that were telling him about the future but now he thought differently. Only day before yesterday he was in the Baidnath Dham Express with his parents returning back to his hometown, when he had dozed off. Only minutes might have passed when he saw a dream where he fell down a steep edge. He had woken up hurriedly. When he tried to get down at the station, he felt a push from back and he fell down right on the platform. He had been thinking Riya's accident only an omen and his falling from the train as well. But Vikas's death made him think now that his dreams were not just omens. They were coming to life. His dreams were becoming real, whatever he saw, everything. So, was it that in a way he was responsible for all that was happening? Was he causing all the accidents?

***

"Why have you come here? Who told you come here?"

Riya was only too furious to see Ritesh standing in front of her. He had brought her favorite fruits and flowers which her father had very generously kept on the table beside the bed. It was already one and Riya's father had brought lunch for her. "Have lunch with us, son," the father said.

Riya began looking the other side. Ritesh said, "oh no, sir, I just came to see her. I have had lunch already." Though he hadn't, he had to lie.

"That's better," Riya murmured.

Ritesh said, "look Riya, I just came to say sorry."

"You don't have to be."

"I left the job. I have come to Bokaro forever."

"Why? I didn't tell you to?"

Ritesh frowned at her ill-behavior but knew she had the right to do so. But he knew this also that she would give in to his persuasions soon. He just would have to keep trying. He returned that day.

Night fell and with it Ritesh felt sleepy too. But never before had he felt such tiredness before. As if the bed was calling him - 'come, I am here for you.' He fell on the bed and went at once into a deep slumber. Thus, his dreams began....

He saw Dr. Mitra and himself at a kachauri stall eating kachauris. They talked happily. The doctor finished his plate early and said - 'okay, Ritesh, I have to go. Important appointment. And thanks for the breakfast' and headed towards the road. Across the road stood his own clinic. Ritesh waved his hand and the doctor waved back. He was still looking behind and walking. He couldn't see the car coming. But Ritesh saw it and he saw it hit the doctor and speed away. The doctor, all bloody, was thrown many metres away from the road. Ritesh ran hurriedly up to him and took him in his arms. The doctor was dead. 'No, no, no,' gasped Ritesh.

"No," Ritesh shrieked as he opened his eyes. He knew it would be the doctor this time and he had to save him, at any cost. It was morning and the doctor would be getting ready to go to work. He would tell him not to leave home today. He dialed the number but even after a long ring, Dr. Mitra didn't pick it up. He dialed again. This time the call was picked.

“Yes, Ritesh, what is it?” the doctor asked.

“Doctor, please, don’t leave for work today,” said Ritesh hurriedly and anxiously, “I saw you in the dream. You had a terrible accident.”

“And you think I will have it really?” said the doctor, “c’mon, Ritesh, you are an intelligent fellow. Don’t talk ridiculous.”

“But...”

“Okay, okay,” said the doctor finally, “anyway my car is at the garage, I will have to walk to the office today. Happy? Now don’t act like my grandma.” Saying so he disconnected the call.

Ritesh sat down on the chair. But the doctor said his car was at the garage and he would walk. The hospital was not very far from his house. Which meant Dr. Mitra had misunderstood him and he was going to the hospital. A car had hit him in the dream, isn’t it? He was walking then. Ritesh dialed the number again. But the doctor didn’t pick it up. Finally, he picked it up on the third ring. “What happened now Ritesh? I am on the road, and I am in a hurry,” the doctor sounded annoyed, “now say fast what.....” but he couldn’t complete his words. Ritesh knew he had been hit.

Next day the newspaper confirmed Ritesh’s guess. It was written clearly in the headlines- ‘famous doctor hit by a car, died on spot.’

***

Ritesh felt he was alone in the world. No one would believe him. He felt he would go mad. He felt he would pluck off all his hair. But what could he do? He tried at least. What more could he do? No, that was no excuse. If something really was going on, he would get to the bottom of it. But where would he start? The pills. Yes, only after the pills he had taken, all the hell had broken lose. It was only after having those damn pills. He still had them with him. He found it in his drawer and looked for its name. Yes, there it was - the name ‘Cure’ was clearly written on it.

Ritesh made an extensive search about the company on the internet. But even after searching for about an hour, he got nothing. He even typed the address in expectation of seeing the company on the maps but only failure came into his account. Finally, he decided giving the company a little visit.

The company, i.e. Cure Chemicals was situated on the outskirts of Hazaribagh. Ritesh had to make a very good reason to his parents as to why he wanted to go there. "An old friend is ill," he had said. As for the company, it was a three storied building and did not look like a pharmaceutical company at all from outside. There was a guard at the front glass door. He asked what he wanted. Ritesh simply said, "I have to say something to the doctors here about the new medicine, that...what's it's name...yeah..." He had never cared to see the name of the new medicine and so he had taken the leaf along with him. He brought it out of his shirt pocket and handed it to the guard. The guard looked suspiciously at him, then took the medicine from his hands. He said, "wait here," and went in. He came out a few minutes later and said, "come with me." Ritesh followed the old man inside the building.

The old guard led Ritesh through a large hall, then by the stairs up to the second floor. On the way he could see other doors both in the hall downstairs and on the second floor, that were closed. Though nothing was written on them, Ritesh guessed they could be the labs or the manufacturing units. The guard went through a hallway and entered a room. Ritesh followed. The room inside looked like some sort of a chemical lab. Two men stood at one corner talking. Both looked of about same age as him. They looked at the guard and Ritesh and one of them said, "ah, you may go Mahesh." The guard nodded and left. Ritesh went up to the two men.

Introductions were done. The two men came to be known as Rajnish Srivastav and Akshay Mathur. Akshay wore glasses. "So, what was it that you wanted to tell us?" asked Rajnish, "seems you have tried our new medicine. How was it?"

Ritesh feared whether to tell his matter or not. Clearly if something really was cooking, they would never accept it. He would have to play the other way. He said, "no, no, I mean I did not take it. It's one of my friends who had fever and the doctor gave him this medicine. Said it was new in the market. He took it, the fever was gone within minutes. He couldn't come so he asked me to thank you personally for such a great work."

The doctors looked at each other for a moment then Akshay said, "and where have you come exactly from?"

"Why? I live here in Hazaribagh," Ritesh lied, "and my friend lives in Ranchi."

"Didn't he tell of any kind of side effect of something?" asked Rajnish worriedly. Ritesh could clearly see the confusion on his face.

"No," he said, "actually he said he had a headache and he felt very sleepy after having the pills."

Both the doctors' faces brightened a little. "That is but natural," said Akshay, "you see, that is a small effect of our pills but that is how it works so well. Anyway, thank you for your time Mr. Ritesh." They shook hands and he was shown outside the lab. But Ritesh was not the person to leave. He pressed his ears by the slightly open door and listened to what the doctors were talking about. Akshay said, "I had told you we should have kept a watch on one of the customers." Rajnish said, "but you saw how it failed here. We tried it on the subject and he had no headaches, no dreams nothing."

That was it. They really were responsible for the dreams. But before Ritesh could do something a hand grabbed at his collar and pushed him inside. It was Mahesh. "He was eavesdropping," he said.

"Ah," said Akshay, "playing the detective, are you?"

"What is really going on here?" asked Ritesh, "what is it about the dreams?"

"Why your friend didn't tell you?" said Rajnish, "didn't he tell you he was having dreams?"

"That became true," completed Ritesh.

"We...," began Akshay, then said, "what? What did you say? True? What do you mean by that?"

"Don't act innocent," said Ritesh, "you people here are conducting some weird tests and making a medicine that will induce sleep over the person and he will have dreams, that will come true and destroy his entire life."

"What rubbish?" said Rajnish annoyed, "we here are conducting tests to see what results come out with our new pills. They induce sleep alright, and he will dream as well but that will only make him want the medicine more. It's a drug and nothing else." With this the two of them took him outside and opened one of the closed doors. Inside was a lab where more people were working with chemicals. Then another door was opened where there were seven people who sat on chairs. They looked like they were in some hypnotic trance. Their eyes were half closed with sleep. Then Akshay said, "you see, these are the subjects, but here we have failed considerably. We were making a medicine that would cure fever as well as induce sleep. Then, in sleep whatever dreams that the subject saw, our aim was to capture the brain signals emitted so that we could know what really he was dreaming about. But the medicine took a wrong turn and it turned into a drug. Our subjects here are wanting more of it. We are working on the cure. Just the final testing is to be done."

Ritesh was totally confused. It was not what he had thought it to be. Rajnish said, "we had released only some medicine in the market, that too to eminent doctors. We wanted the test to go successful but then this happened. We then stopped the medicine and informed the doctors only yesterday not to give the medicine to anyone."

Ritesh decided to leave. If this was the matter then what was it that was happening with him? He came back home and thought profusely about it but without success. Then something got into his brain. Why hadn't he observed this before? He had seen the doctor and his friend die in the dream, so they were dead. But he had woken up just when Riya had been hit by the truck, so she had suffered only a fracture. It his dreams were the ones that were causing all this, then it was possible that he could change their course. He could try at least.

***

Night fell and sleep took Ritesh into its arms again. As was obvious, he began dreaming. This time he saw Riya's father walking on the road. He had his satchel of vegetables for his hotel. Ritesh was also there on the other side of the road. He stood there watching him. But even in the dream he knew something would happen any moment now. He had to be ready. A speeding car came from behind. The old man was not aware of it. The car's brakes seemed to have failed. Everyone on the road moved away from it but he didn't. Ritesh ran out to him and pulled him aside just in time as the car passed very close by him. With this his sleep broke. Ritesh was satisfied with himself but then, he would have to test whether Riya's father was really alright. For this he would have to go to the hospital.

Riya lay as usual on her bed while her father opened the tiffin box for lunch. Ritesh was only too happy to see him. He hurriedly went up to him and hugged him tight. "What happened, son?" asked the confused man.

"Oh, nothing, it's just that I saw a bad dream about you," said Ritesh. Riya couldn't help smiling. And Ritesh marked that.

"Oh," said her father, "what luck I had. This morning, a car, which was coming from the back, had its brakes failed. A young man pulled me aside so I was saved. Or else..."

Ritesh hugged him again. He had understood the game. If he couldn't resist sleep and the dreams from coming, at least he could divert the effect. As far as the medicine was concerned, he would take them for now. He would see if the dreams stopped on stopping the medicine. But that would be later on.

Ritesh sat up in bed. His t-shirt was stuck to his body due to sweat. It was still dark outside the window. He looked at the clock. It struck one. What a terrible dream. He had seen his parents this time. He got out of bed and went straight into their room. In the dark he could make out the faint outline of his father. They were inside their blankets. He went up to them. An unknown fear grudged him as he tried to remove the blankets. With a jerk he removed them finally and gasped with horror. Two skeletons lay in place of his parents.

"No," he shrieked and sat up in bed. What? What was that? A dream? A dream inside a dream. He was panting and was covered in sweat. He looked outside his window. It was dark.

His eyes fell on the clock. It struck one. He opened the bottle on the side table and drank the whole water in one go. Suddenly he realized something. Apart from drinking the water, everything had happened in the same manner. He got out of his bed and went straight into his parents' room. He didn't wait, just rushed in and removed the blankets from his parents. But at once he had to pray why did he do so? "No, no, no," he cried, "no." He sat down beside the bed on the floor and looked at the skulls as they stared back at him with their hollow eyes.

****

CHAPTER VIII

THE PARTY

She sat at the door, fearful of his forceful entry and covered her mouth by her palms, in case he heard her sobs. Tears rolled down her eyes continuously and hiccups at regular intervals made her muffled sobs only louder. Her long shoulder level hair fell loosely all over like some mad person and her makeup had worn off due to the tears. The kohl of her eyes was on all over her cheeks now and the strawberry flavored lipstick was smeared all over her mouth. Her body shivered, not due to cold, but due to fear. She could hear the shoe steps on the stairs. He was coming. The loud blaring of music downstairs came till here. Her flailing majenta skirt and red top were torn from parts and her body was scratched from many places. Shikha Talwar, you are doomed, she said again and again to herself. Why did she ever agree to come to this party? Oh yes, her best friend Nitu had persuaded her to come along. "We will have fun," she had said, "now don't be a bore." The girl, whom every other girl thought to be the coolest and every boy thought to be hottest in the college, Sneha Mehra had thrown a party for her birthday at her farm house in a sprawling 30 acres land situated on the outskirts of the city and invited all her friends. Needless to say, the whole college was her friend. And she was rich. Her father was in export-import business - all the more reason to waste money. Whatever it was, when it came upon attending a party of the most popular girl in college, you had to wear the most coolest dresses. Shikha hadn't thought her new skirt and top would make her fall into such danger.

A sound made Shikha look here and there - had he entered the room from some other way? No, there was no one. The sound had come from outside. Shoes. He had reached to the top and was now perhaps wandering which room could it be. There were four other rooms on this floor and all the doors were closed. He would have to open and see in every room. She hadn't even asked him his name. When she first met him in the party tonight, he looked quite charming and talked nice things too. He was some cousin of Sneha who had come from some other place. She didn't remember the place - her head still swung from the drink. She had just cut herself off from the dance floor for a while when he had approached her for a drink. She had politely refused. He offered her orange juice then. Orange juice was okay. But she did not realize he had mixed something in it. She had felt dizzy after drinking it. He said he would take care of her and helped her and took her to another room, that was empty of course.

This room had only a sleeping mattress. Her head was reeking of pain

and she had thrown herself on the bed. Only then she had realized a palm moving over her thigh. The boy was very close to her and his hand was caressing her skin. She had tried to gather herself, tried to get away, but her swinging head did not allow her to. "It's okay," he had said and then he had kept his lips on hers. Only when the kiss went up to their heads, she had felt his fingers tugging at her top. The dizziness had broken for a moment and she had pushed him aside. "What are you doing?" she had almost shouted. Just then Sneha had entered the room and saw them. But she had only smiled at them and said to the boy, "okay, so now you are good?" He had winked at her and showed a thumbs up. "Okay, then, I will leave the two of you. Have fun," she had said and left, closing the door behind her. The coolest girl had left her to be molested by her cousin, huh? Not so cool after all. She got up to go, but he had grabbed her wrist and tried to pull her. But she had kicked him in the stomach and made for the door. After that what happened made her shiver. He had dashed and grabbed her by her waist, lifting her in air. Tugging at her clothes and in the course, tearing them. She had struggled hard, trying to free herself and fighting him. She had succeeded in in freeing herself and made for the door again, this time coming out of the room. Only she made a wrong turn. She had to move towards the party, where there were her other friends, but she made for the stairs. Her dizzy head had showed her the wrong way. And this she realized only when she had entered this old, vacant room and locked the door.

Why had she even agreed to come to this damn party? She thought again. She had come to this city to study, to make something out of her life, she had fought with her parents to take admission to this college as Nitu was coming here as well. Nitu was her childhood friend and she did not want to lose her. Her father had told her so many times that if she had to study in some private institute then there were better colleges than this engineering college, why to invest in a college that had been inaugurated only three years ago. But she had not listened. And now she was in such a big trouble. Suddenly there was a knock on the door. "I know, you are in here, baby." The words fell like acid in her ears. He had found her. God, now what would she do? Suddenly she felt a push. He was pushing the door. He was trying to brake it open. She stood up and pushed at the door herself, to stop it from braking open. But there was no match for a frail girl, who was already exhausted from the last minutes' struggle and whose head was still going dizzy due to the drink with someone whose adrenaline charged him fully. The door broke open and she was thrown on the floor. He stood at the door, the lights behind him made him a dark figure making him look like a monster. "Tch...tch...tch...," he said, "look at yourself. What will happen if you agree to me?"

"Don't come near me," she screamed but he had closed the door now.

"Scream all you want, there's no one gonna hear you, darling," he said and began approaching. She tried to get up and run but he was upon her now. She did not have the least strength left. He grabbed her by her waist and made her lie on her back, then locked her hands on the floor. "Please, please, let me go," she began crying. But the monster only smiled.

***

Two years have passed since the incident. She stood in front of the same farm house now. This house remained vacant most of the time of the year. There were other houses too in this area but this one was a little aloof from the others - having a yard of its own and the trees all around it gave it a shadowy environment. It was very near to the institute as well. Only when it was that Mr. Mehra, Sneha's father had to spend some time alone, he would come here, or it was some big smashing party of Sneha or some silent professional party of her father when he had made a profit in business. These were the only times this three storey bungalow would see people, else, it was the sole property of the caretaker himself. He was an old man, around fifty, with big moustache and wore dhoti and an extra large shirt and always had a cane with him. He stood there at the gates right now. Perhaps he was waiting for someone to come. She stood by some bushes and watched. This year would be the final year of her B.Tech course. She could get a job then? Get settled? But no.

Suddenly the sound of screeching tires caught her attention and she became extra cautious. A jeep stood at the door and on it sat Sneha, two other boys and two other girls. One of the boys was the same, Sneha's cousin, the monster of two years ago. The other one was Sunny, a guy from the electrical branch. Who were the two other girls? She narrowed her eyes and tried to look clearly. One of them she could not recognize. The other one - wait, was it Nitu? Yes, it was Nitu. What was she doing with them? They all looked happy. And they waved beer bottles in their hands.

Naturally something very good had happened so there was some reason for these bastards to party? But why was Nitu with them? She meant to find out.

***

"Behold, guys," said Sneha in a tone like that of a host, "you are about to enter the haunted farm house that belongs to Sneha Mehra."

"Haunted? Huh?" said Nitu, looking at the face of the other girl who was getting nervous now, "and why do you call it that? I mean, we have been here before to party and all has been fine."

"Dear," said Sneha, coming closer to Nitu, "I don't say it. But other people do. You know what? My father had thrown a party only three months ago for his associates, and you know what happened?"

"What?" everyone said in unison.

"I don't know? I was not there to see," said Sneha, smiling, then getting very serious suddenly, "but the people in the party did not have a very pleasant experience here. They say, the current had been off for about three hours and some of them even saw dark figures lurking at the stairs and in the balcony."

"Huh? Figures?" said her cousin, "surely they were other party attenders?"

"Party people?" said Sneha, "no, Abhishek, they weren't. People saw those figures appearing and disappearing in the dim lights."

There was a pause for a while. Nobody said anything. Then Sunny broke the silence, "you can't frighten me. You are making up the story. And even if there are ghosts lurking here, we shall see to them."

"That's very brave of you Sunny," said Sneha, "I hope too that there are some ghosts in here. Or else the night would get spoiled and we won't be able to see your bravery against them. Okay, now let's party, guys. It's our recruitment day tonight. Our college has given us jobs today."

With that everyone began shrieking and hooting and Sneha put on the music. "Everyone, to the floor," called Sneha, holding a beer bottle in hand and shaking her body. The nervous girl still stood on the side, watching everyone dance when Nitu saw her. She went up to her, grabbed her hand and pulled her saying, "oh, come on, Nargis, you are our junior doesn't mean you can't enjoy. You are our friend, and behave like one." Nargis reluctantly joined the group and soon became accustomed to the dance. The music played in full blast.

It was about an hour later when the window suddenly opened with a loud bang. This made the girls shriek and the boys were obviously surprised. Then Sneha said, "oh, it's just the window. I will get it." She walked up to it and closed it. "There, now don't open and freak us out, okay," she said as if scolding the window.

Sunny said, "I would have a drink." And moved out of the party. He came to the counter and poured beer in a glass. Slowly the others too came out from the dance space. They all needed a little brake. They chatted and drank happily away and discussed all sorts of things - from what was in menu today to what everyone would do next in life. Meanwhile, Sneha called the caretaker and handed him the food packets ordering him to get them warmed. The caretaker took the packets and went away.

By and by Abhishek glanced only at Nargis and tried to talk only to her. She was beautiful not only by face but by body too, as he observed. Her long black hair fell loosely from one side of her shoulder and a brown streak of lock dangled in front. She wore a dazzling black thigh length dress and high heels. He soon got into conversation with her and offered her a drink. Nargis was into beer and happily drank down the glass provided. Abhishek smiled, everything was going as he planned.

Half an hour more passed. The caretaker didn't bring the food yet. Sneha began to grow anxious. "I will get this caretaker fired," she murmured and went out of the room to see him. Meanwhile Sunny chatted with Nitu.

"How surprising we have never talked earlier," said Sunny.

"Yeah, really," replied Nitu, shyly. Both had checked each other out for some time now, but never got a chance as this to talk. They used to only glance at each other in college. 'Hi's and 'Hello's only. The attraction had naturally grown up.

Meanwhile Nargis began feeling uneasy as the beer had gone up to her head and Abhishek had come much closer to her than before. He had even clasped her palm. She freed herself saying, "I need to go to the washroom."

"Shall I help you?" he asked.

"No, no," she said, "I can manage." And she walked off for the washroom. Perhaps she was aware of Abhishek's intentions. She entered the bathroom and closed the door. The bathroom with its large space and five taps with a long basin and a large mirror looked as if it had come right from some five star hotel. Needless to say who its owner was. She opened a tap and splashed water at her face again and again. She closed it and looked herself in the mirror, when she had to shriek with fear. There was someone else in it staring at her.

***

Nargis turned to see who it was. A girl, a year or two older than her, she wore a top and skirt and her hair fell loose on her back. It was Shikha, though Nargis didn't know her. "Who...who are you?" she asked fearfully.

"Don't be afraid," said Shikha, "I am a classmate of Nitu, her friend."

"But you didn't come with us? How did you enter this house?"

Shikha smiled. Then said, "that's not a problem stupid. Problem is... Abhishek."

"Abhishek?" said Nargis, "what of him?"

"Don't fall for him," said her senior, "he is a bastard. He cheated me as well. He will just..."

Shikha's words were cut off by the knocks on the door. It was Abhishek. "Hey, Nargis," he called, "are you alright? Shall I call the doctor?"

Nargis began to go when Shikha said again, "get out of the party as soon as possible and go home."

Nargis rubbed the water on her face and came out. "What happened dear? Why so late? You alright?" said Abhishek putting his palm on her shoulder but she

moved her shoulder away and said, "yeah, I am fine."

"Whom were you talking to?" he said trying to look inside.

But Nargis was far smarter. She said, "so you keep eyeing girls, don't you, what they are doing in the washroom."

Abhishek was flustered. "Ah...no no," he said, "it's just that, when I came to see you I heard some noises inside."

"Let's go," said she and walked away. Abhishek followed.

Sneha came to the kitchen but could not see the caretaker anywhere. The kitchen was a large place too, like some big restaurant with a marble table in the middle to cook. The food packets were kept on it. She looked all around and yes, there in the corner lay someone with his face down. Surely it was the caretaker. Sneha fearfully went up to him and turned him on his back. But she had to gasp and move away with horror. Blood was gushing out of his forehead.

***

Today Abishek's plans were going to waste, perhaps fate didn't want his wish to get fulfilled - he cursed when the glass of wine in which he had mixed a pill secretly and that he offered to Nargis fell down on its own when she kept it on the table. The wine spread all over. Abhishek cursed again because now he wasn't getting the other pills he had kept in his jacket pocket. He cursed again because when he went up to the vodka bottle, it was not there. It lay on the floor, shattered to pieces with the vodka all over the floor. 'Damn,' he thought, 'what's happening tonight.' Finally he thought he wouldn't use any means now. And by the way, the pill had no effect on that Shikha girl two years ago. All he thought now that he would use his charm over Nargis and if it failed, force was always an option.

So now he kept himself always close to Nargis and talked to her with all the affection he could. Nargis slowly realized why he was becoming so flirtatious. Perhaps the girl in the bathroom was right. She tried to keep her cool and decided she would leave at the right opportunity. But the right opportunity was nowhere to be seen. Nitu was busy with Sunny across the table and wasn't even looking at Nargis. Finally she moved away from Abhishek and said, "I will go now."

"What?" said Abhishek, "not so soon. Have dinner first. I wonder where did this Sneha go now." Nargis had to wait. She tried again but Abhishek agreed her in to stay. But half an hour passed and Sneha still was nowhere to be seen. Abhishek decided this was the moment. He came closer to Nargis and whispered in her ear, "you are so beautiful, you know that?"

Nargis became uneasy. Remain away, away, her mind screamed, don't give in. "I will leave now, I think," she said and began to go when Abhishek held her wrist, "come, you are not feeling well here. We will talk somewhere else." And he pulled her to one corner of the hall where there was another door to go to an attached room. She tried to free herself but couldn't. Abhishek pushed her to the wall and locked both his hands around her. He approached her to kiss. But she moved her head away, "what are you doing?" Then she looked over to Nitu and called, "Nitu. Please, let's go."

But Nitu was not at all in the mood to leave. Though she was not drunk, still, perhaps the company of Sunny was more alcoholic than any liquor to her. "Oh, have fun Nargis," she said, "don't be a bore. This is the time to have fun." From behind another window, Shikha watched. Was it Nitu, her best friend? Was she really talking like this? Instead of taking Nargis home, when she could really see what was happening? Nargis had no way out. She was like a bird captured in a cage. The girl in the bathroom was right. She knew what Abhishek wanted, but it was late now. He had pressed his mouth over her lips. She struggled and pushed him away. But he was stronger. He held her wrist, opened the door, and pushed her inside. Then he came in too and locked the door behind. He smiled, his eyes shined with monstrosity. "You really are beautiful, so sad you didn't have a boyfriend," he said.

"You are crossing your limits, Abhishek," she said and tried to go past him but he blocked her path and pushed her on the bed. He got on the bed and upon her. She struggled but he locked her hands to the bed. Tears rolled down her eyes. "Ah...don't cry, baby," he said, "it will take only a few minutes."

But fate wasn't really with him tonight. Or perhaps there was someone else standing in between his fate and him. Suddenly, as if someone pulled him by his leg and he fell down on the floor and was pulled away from the bed. He looked here and there, surprised. Nargis sat up. There in front of the bed stood the girl, from the bathroom. And at whom Abhishek was staring with horrified eyes.

As if he had seen death itself. "You, you," he stammered, "you ....can't..."

"You are a dog, Abhishek, a monster," Shikha said, "you destroyed my life and now you were going to destroy hers?"

"No...no....,"Abhishek stammered, "you can't....be..."

Nargis was confused as to why Abhishek was so terrified. Suddenly the lights went out and there was total darkness. There was a blood curdling shriek of Abhishek. After a few seconds there were knocks on the door and voices of Sunny and Nitu on the other side. They were calling Abhishek's and Nargis' names and were trying to open the door. Nargis realized they tried to push it open, but the door wouldn't budge. She was terrified and tears rolled continuously from her eyes. Suddenly the door opened and Nitu and Sunny came in. The lights came to and what everyone saw made them shiver. There on the floor lay Abhishek, with an iron rod going right through his chest. There was blood all over the floor. He was dead. Nitu and Nargis shrieked with horror while Sunny didn't know what to do. "What happened here?" he asked.

"What will you do by knowing." The feminine voice came from across the room. But there was no one else in the room. "The girl," said Nargis, "she killed him."

Suddenly the lights began going dim again. There was a sound of something metal and Sunny shrieked. There was a window and some light was now entering through it. Nargis could clearly see the feminine figure standing with a rod, across the room. Sunny lay on the floor, unconscious. 'She, she killed him," cried Nargis again, "she....saved me from Abhishek."

Nitu stared at her friend with the same horror with which Abhishek was looking. "This can't be....," she said.

"What happened, Nitu?" asked Nargis. Fear gripped her but somehow she knew this girl would not harm her.

"Hello, Nitu," said Shikha, "missed me?"

Nitu's eyes went wide with horror. She shrieked and sat down on the floor. Nargis sat near her too. "She is here to help us," she said.

"But she is dead," cried Nitu with tears in her eyes, "she was dead two

years ago, damn it. She commited suicide by jumping from this same building when Abhishek molested her."

Now Nargis knew why Shikha was here, how she got here, why she was there in the washroom, the secret behind the story of the ghosts Sneha was talking about. She looked at Shikha. She was smiling. Nitu had fainted. She felt dizzy too. Her eyes closed.

***

When her eyes opened, Nargis found herself on a bed in a hospital room. She looked all around wearily and saw Sunny sitting on a stool. He had bandage wrapped around his forehead. When he saw Nargis, he came near her. "What happened?" she asked.

"Don't ask," he said, "when I gained my senses, I saw you and Nitu unconscious. I went to look for Sneha and found the caretaker unconscious and Sneha dead."

"What? Dead?" came out of Nargis' mouth.

"A rod went in through her chest just like Abhishek. Then I called the police," said Sunny, "now you say, what had happened after I fainted."

"Her name was Shikha," she said, "she saved me from Abhishek. But Nitu was saying she was dead?"

Sunny sighed. He told her the sad story of Shikha Talwar. How Nitu had brought her to the party and how Abhishek had raped her and she had committed suicide by jumping from the terrace. And there was no way she could return. Abhishek was a rich brat and his father had filled the officers' mouth with money then. There had been no case - only this, that the girl was drunk and had slipped and fell off the roof. Nitu was unconscious after her treatment and the doctors said she would come into senses by the next day. The police was there too but they didn't believe in the story of a ghost haunting the group. They made it a case of infiltration and theft. They said it was the whims and fancies of the young people that they saw a ghost. They believed the liqor had got high on them. They even decided, the kids also might be taking drugs, because some antidepressants were actually found in Sneha's purse.

Next day Sunny and Nargis went to see Nitu. "I don't know what was the fault of Sneha in this," said Nargis on the way.

"Fault? You know, what," said Sunny, "when Abhishek was trying on Shikha, Sneha had seen them, but did not stop Abhishek. In a way she had helped him. And I have heard there had been a deal between Abhishek and Nitu. He had asked her to bring Shikha to the party, because Nitu and Shikha were room-mates, living on rent. And in return he had made her pass in the exams. You know how rich people are. They can show money anywhere."

The doctor said it would not be good to see her. She had gained her senses but she was not unto herself. They looked from the glass window on the door. Nitu sat there beside the wall and had a pencil in her hand. There was something written all over the wall. Nargis read it - 'I took her to the party.'

"We might have to admit her to the mental asylum," said the doctor and went away.

"Supporting a crime makes you equally shared in it," said Sunny.

Nargis looked at Nitu for the last time. She had taken her too along in the party. She wondered what deal she had made this time with Abhishek. She watched and a tear rolled down from her eye as Nitu continuously wrote on the wall about her guilt. Then she turned and walked away.

CHAPTER IX

MESSAGES

That day I met some of my school friends at The Delight at the main market. It was the birthday of one called Sunil and he had decided to spend the day with us. Meeting old friends and having a nice chat with biriyani on the table, that too in the city where we all had grown up together, what more could one want? We were five of us present and another one was on his way. “Ajit is always late,” complained Sunil grumpily.

“Don’t take it so hard,” said Malini keeping a hand on his shoulder, “probably he got stuck in some work. Moreover, our cake has not yet come as well.” Since it was a birthday party, in spite of Sunil’s preventive requests, we had ordered for a cake. “After all, we have met after such a long time,” Malini had said. It was a good idea after all. Since leaving school years ago, we all had taken our own paths, looking towards our careers. And after almost 9 long years, we had met in our same old place where we hung out then, to remember those days again.

“Speaking of the devil, he is here,” said Manasi pointing at the door of the restaurant. There stood our pal Ajit, but he looked as if he had got thinner than before. Moreover, I hadn’t seen him for a while and had now come to forget his face even. Ajit came up to us and took his seat. He wore jeans and a jacket. “Why are you wearing jacket? It’s not that cold,” said Rama who herself was wearing a sweater.

“Look, who is talking,” I said, mockingly, “Miss Sweater.” We got into a chat and talked all sorts of things. This was getting excited. The arrival of the cake made things greater. We even made a plan to go to the movies after lunch. Sunil agreed to pay for it as well, as he had got a promotion only recently and he said it was his birthday too.

Sunil cut the cake, the ceremonies were done, the cake was finished,

soon after which the biriyanis arrived and we began eating. But I noticed Ajit looked nervous. He ate like someone who was amidst strangers and would jump if someone told him something. I asked, "something happened to you?"

"Don't ask," he said.

"Hey, our friend has a secret," said Rama, "c'mon, Ajit, tell us. We are old friends, right?"

"No, no, it's nothing," said Ajit, but his face screamed out loud that he had a secret. He had to agree finally when everyone began coaxing him. But he said, "remember, you are listening to this at your own risk."

"We will see to that," said Sunil.

Ajit cleared his throat and began, "first tell me, who here believes in ghosts, spirits, or any such sort. Supernatural, paranormal or aliens or any such thing."

There was no one in our group that believed in that kind of stuff. Though we liked movies of the mentioned genre. And the movie we were about to go was one such too. Ajit began again, "I didn't believe in them too. But...."

"But?" asked Malini anxiously. She was a lot into these. Horror novels, movies, soaps and serials were her favorites.

"Something happened," said Ajit, "and I now believe in them."

"So what happened?" I asked.

Ajit looked at me, then at others, then said again, "I was at my cousin's marriage ceremony a few days ago at Gaya. My parents could not go, so I was to represent them in the procession, that was to begin from Dhanbad - where he lives. I was sitting in the bus quietly. Most of the people were my cousin's friends and I knew none of them. So, I decided to spend the 5 hour journey all by myself. I had taken a window seat and there I sat quietly, staring at others. You know how I am, I don't mingle with relatives that much."

"Yeah," said Sunil, "you have always been like that. Then what happened?"

Ajit continued, "the bus started at four in the afternoon. We were to reach Gaya around nine or something, eat and return. The journey was long and I began feeling bored after the first hour passed. The people who were acquainted with each other were having a nice time but poor me was a big bore. There was another man sitting beside me. He was elder than me and sat quietly as well. I began talking to him anyway. We introduced each other and talked all sorts of things. That man came out to be a maternal uncle of my cousin. He was not so old in age, to be anyone's uncle especially when that someone is only two or three years younger than him, but you know how it goes in a village. You have uncles and aunts who are even younger than you."

"Yes, you know, I have a relative in the village and she happens to be my mother's aunt," said Rama, excitedly, "and she is even younger than me."

"Hmm...Even I have a grandfather who is younger than my father," said Sunil.

Ajit looked at his 'disturbing agents' and said, "now, can I complete my story?"

"Ah... yes, yes," said Sunil.

"So, we talked and talked," said Ajit, "and my time passed quite nicely. But then, at around eight the bus broke down. it was somewhere near IT square. The driver said something was wrong in the engine and he would have to look at it. It would take some time. Since it was a procession, the other bus that was right behind us had to stop too. It was already around 8 and people were getting annoyed. Luckily there was a roadside dhaba nearby, so the people who felt

hungry decided to help themselves.

"My new friend, whose name was Shankar, asked me if I would join him for a light snack at least. He reasoned this by saying, 'who knows when we will reach now?' I thought this to be a good idea and we took a table. Then I saw what Shankar meant by a little snack.

He ordered four naans and a full plate of chicken masala for himself. I asked him how could he eat so much when there was food at the marriage reception. He reasoned this by saying again, 'who knows when we will reach Ajit ji, and moreover, you should do what your mind tells you to.' I agreed and decided to have only an omlette for myself.

"While we ate, the driver came and said that he could take a little while more. It could get late, so he asked us to rest in the dhaba itself. Shankar said he had come to the place before and there were large halls made with chaukis for truck drivers, especially who drove all day and stopped at such places to rest at night. Many people retired to the halls that were made at the back of the hotel. Many people just roamed about to enjoy the cold breeze. Shankar and I decided to take a little rest. We found one isolated small room with a chauki, one of the wall's of which was broken at the corner making a small space to go outside. Shankar closed his eyes at once but the space in the broken wall caught my attention. I got up and walked up to it. I peeped outside. There was nothing except darkness. I came out of the room and saw there were bricks and sand kept on the side. Perhaps the hotel owner was about to reconstruct the wall. And then I saw it. The thing that changed my views about the unknown."

"What was it?" asked Manav asked.

Ajit smiled. Rama said, "oh! Don't create suspense. Just complete the story."

Ajit nodded and began, "it was a piece of metal. Ordinary, like it might have come out or broken from some machine or something. It was rhombic in shape and a little bent. I picked it up to examine it. Naturally I wanted to know what kind of a machine it was part of. But as I examined it all over, I could not guess what it was. Suddenly my phone vibrated. A message had come. I took it out and saw what was written. It was written- 'keep it down.'

"Obviously, I didn't understand a bit of it. I just kept it back in my pocket and went back to my examining. After five minutes my phone vibrated again. Another message. I read it again and this time

I knew what it meant - ‘keep it down, it’s not yours.’ I looked all around. There was no one. Outside as well as inside. Shankar was asleep and moreover we hadn’t exchanged numbers. So, he could not have sent the message. Then I decided to look at the number and I was shocked. There was no number written.”

“What?” asked Rama, anxiously.

“Hey, you don’t have to give that horror movie expression, okay,” said Manav.

“What do you mean by there was no number written,” I said, “I mean

there are softwares and cell phones today in the market that don’t show any number but write ‘unknown number’ on the screen but there are options to see...”

My words weren’t even complete when Ajit kept his mobile phone on the table. It was a simple Nokia classic. “It shows all numbers, alright? When a call from an unknown number comes, it shows the number,” said Ajit, then again, he kept it back in his pocket and said, “but when those messages came, there was no number written. So, I naturally became a little disturbed. I again looked here and there but there was no one. Then there was another message and this time it was written - ‘why are you looking here and there? Keep the thing down. It’s not yours.’

“The metal piece dropped from my hand. I understood the messages were for me and there was something, some power that was the owner of the metal piece and he didn’t want me to touch it. Suddenly I heard Shankar calling my name. I looked inside from the wall. He informed that the driver had called. The bus had been repaired. I told him to go and I would just come. Then I picked up the artifact, put it in my pocket and came out of the place. But, as long as I walked the few metres to the bus, my phone kept vibrating continuously. Fear gripped me so much that I didn’t dare to look at the phone. I knew ‘he’ was sending me the messages. Then I sat on my seat beside Shankar. He asked me what I was up to. I didn’t tell him the matter. The bus started and we happily reached the reception. I didn’t get any message again. But it left quite an impact on me."

There was a pause for a moment. We all looked at each other, then, at Ajit. He looked at everyone and sighed. Then he asked, "what, you don't believe me?"

Rama picked up her hand like a small kid in a school and said, "I believe

you." Sunil looked at her and sighed.

Manav said, "look pal, it's a strange story, but..."

"There's no logic, you see," said Malini.

"There might have been kids playing pranks on you," said Manav.

Ajit shook his head, "and how do you explain the unnumbered messages?"

"You said you had taken the artifact with you, didn't you?" I said. Ajit nodded his head. I said again, "can you show it?"

Ajit said, "I knew you people won't believe me. So, I have brought it along." Saying so he took out a piece of blue metal from his jacket.

"Awesome," said Rama, wide eyed, "that's why you were wearing the jacket, to carry it."

He put the metal on the table. It was not very big, but big enough to be

the size of a cell phone. It was exactly as our friend had described. We all touched it, examined it in turn. "You didn't get any messages when you took it along, right?" I said.

"Yes," he said.

"That proves someone was playing a prank on you, a very big prank," I declared.

Ajit was about to say something when his phone vibrated again. He took it out and saw. "Now whose message..." he murmured reading the message and as soon as he did it his eyes went wide with terror. The phone fell from his shivering hands and he stood up and darted out of the restaurant. "Stop, Ajit," I cried but he was gone. Suddenly there was a blood curdling shriek that came from outside the restaurant along with sound of crashing and brakes screeching.

Rama picked up the cell phone and we darted out of the hotel too. There on the road lay a crushed Ajit in a pool of blood, dead and a car, a few yards from him. People were gathering around the scene. Rama looked at the phone and shrieked. We all looked at her. She showed us the message on the phone. There was the message - 'you think you are smart to touch the thing and take it along with you? Now you show it to your friends. Alright, now see what happens to you and your friends.' And there was no number to this message.

****

CHAPTER X

THAT NIGHT

It was a heavy downpour. Now, the big bullet like drops of rain have turned into thin strings of drizzle but the wind makes it no less than its former form. At parts, the road looks as if a boat would be required to cross it. The street light is glowing dimly. A man stands beside it. He has been standing there since the last one hour. He has downed a black raincoat that is completely drenched now. The hood is pulled over his head hiding most of his facial expressions. He looks around him. There is no one except a dog a few feet away. It is staring at him for some time now. Suddenly it begins to bark. It barks twice then slows down to low whining. That's good, he thinks, he wouldn't like it if anyone saw him. Across the street stand a series of blocks. It's already 11.30. Not a single light is on. That's the way it goes in this small town. Even the most populated areas of such places also don't care to wake up till late. Cars are parked in front of some houses, but most of them are in the garages just in front of the buildings across the thin road. A smile comes on the thin lips of the man at the thought of the vulnerability of these vehicles. In the past it would not have been more than a piece of cake for him to steal any one of these, that are standing out in the rain, whichever he chose. Yes, the ones in the garages would give him some challenge. But now, he has left the job. He has left everything. The reason resides in the ground floor flat of the building in front of him just across the road. He will meet her today.

Inside the house, it is total darkness. There is a hall in the middle that is the path to go to the two rooms on the right side. Another door opens to the kitchen. There is a fireplace under a mantelpiece on the opposite side. A fire burns with its own queer voice. A woman sits comfortably on a rocking chair, knitting a sweater. Two locks fall over her face while the rest of her hair is tied in a knot. She is wearing a blue colored gown. She groans once at the thought of the electricity failure of the area due to the rain. But the rain is only an excuse of the municipality. This locality is the most populated area of the city and problems of electricity and water are prominent. Now-a-days the coming of the electricity becomes an occasion of happiness for people. There is a knock on the door. But the door is already open. The woman looks as the door is pushed and a man in a black raincoat standing is visible. But this doesn't worry the woman one bit. The same calmness persists on her face. It is as if she had been waiting for him.

"Still keeping the door open?" The man says as he gets in and opens his dripping raincoat. Then he looks here and there for a nail and finally finding one, hangs it on the wall.

"Finally, you learnt some etiquette?" the woman says.

"Hello Cathleen," he says.

"Hello Alex," she replies.

***

The fire is still burning. Rumbling in the clouds can still be heard. Alex sits in front of the fire on the floor, bathing his fists with the comforting heat. He has defied the woman's trial to offer him a chair. He is wearing a blue shirt and a pair of denims. "You have changed a lot," says Cathleen observing his dirty clothes. They are the same he had worn when he had left her.

"Changed?" Alex is a little confused.

"You have turned more decent, more calm, more...," Cathleen stops at short fall of words.

"Wise?" Alex completes her.

"Yeah, may be."

Alex chuckles, "they teach you what's necessary. Like you always said - 'grow up'."

And with this Cathleen's eyes go to her days only two years back when she had met Alex. She was in search of a job, then, as a teacher or something, though she had decided it would be just to pass her time. Finally she had to get married to some person her father would decide. Until then she could at least live as per her own terms. That day she was at the Harsha Plaza mall with her friend when suddenly she felt a violent push from behind. She fell on her stomach with another person upon her back. This man was Alex who was frolicking with his friends when one of them had pushed him deliberately on her. He helped her up with profuse apologies while she kept on murmuring names. Alex then went on his games while Cathleen said to her friend, “some people never grow.”

Now, Cathleen smiles at this thought and says, “so, how are you Alex?”

There is a pause. Alex stares at the fire without blinking and Cathleen knows that he is also thinking about their past. A past that is filled with love, joy and... blood. Alex had observed the young woman very carefully upon whom he had fallen in the mall and he had decided to meet her. Anyhow. And finally after a lot of search and research he found her house. But he didn’t get the guts to go and speak to her. He didn’t even know her name. So, he stalked her for a few days. Saw what she did, where she went, observed every movement and finally one morning he got his chance.

She was at the library. He took a book too and sat just beside her. Before he could begin, to his great surprise, the girl began herself. She said, “I have seen you. You have been following me for quite some time. Why?”

Her words took him by surprise. He said, “why? What why?”

“Why are you following me? And I remember, you are the man who had fallen upon me in the mall. So? Why are you following me?”

Alex had no answer. He kept silent. Then he said again, “I want to know your name.”

“Why?”

“You have so many questions,” he said, irritated, “can’t I know your name?”

Cathleen smiled, “no. Not without reason.”

It was then that he had proposed to her. But this too he had said as if he was doing some charity. He said, “because I like you. Is this reason enough for you?”

Alex and Cathleen both smile. They look at each other and Alex says, "those days were really something." Suddenly there is a noise of breaking glass that startles Alex. He says, "what was that?"

"Nothing," says Cathleen, "must be the cat. It has a habit of breaking something."

Cathleen had not accepted him the same moment, obviously. But his way of approaching her so out rightly had clearly impressed her. So, she had given him time. They had become friends first. They passed time with each other. They went to the movies, had dinner, went to all the sight-seeing places in town. Gradually she grew a soft corner for him as well. And just like a fairy tale, friendship turned to love. Love for Cathleen had always been a fairy tale thing. She had always thought of her marriage to some stranger with whom she would have to spend all her life. She believed she would find her prince charming in that stranger. But when love knocked at her door, she couldn't resist herself from inviting it in. And finally, one day that which would have been a taboo for Cathleen also happened. Her parents were out of town for a day and she was at Alex's house - this house. She hadn't yet told her parents about him. Alex lived alone, he had no family. The same conditions as tonight had emerged then as well. It was raining heavily and Cathleen had to stop. It was getting dark and Alex ignited the fire. Suddenly there was a loud rumble and the lights went out. The loud rumble made Cathleen grab Alex. The flames within the hearts had grown as well. They kissed. The gown came down, shirt was pulled away and the first making of love took place in front of the same fire where the couple is now sitting.

"We can never get those days back," says Cathleen.

"Why? What?" Alex says. He is a little confused at what he has heard. "Why are you saying like that? I know it has been late, but see, I have returned after all." Suddenly there is another sound, like that of a footstep but Alex doesn't bother about that much.

Cathleen smiles half-heartedly. "First, you say yourself that it has been late and then again you say you have returned. How ironic Alex," she says.

Alex stares at her face for a while. That same beauty has been maintained since the last time he had seen her. Only she looks fairer now. Or maybe it's just the fire that is making her face glow. He smiles. "Look, I know you have gone through a lot, but..." but he cannot finish his line because Cathleen begins herself, "gone through a lot.... That is what you have to say, yes? Gone through a lot." Alex remains silent. She needs to take her anger out. He deserves at least that much. Cathleen says, "you know, Alex, very well, that I had gone against my father to be with you...." And her voice brakes, it is full.

She had taken Alex to her father a few days after their union and said she wanted to marry him. Her father slapped her and did not say a word. She went in, came out with a bag and Alex brought her to his house. Her father did not even care to stop her, while her mother wept all the time.

"What did you give me in return, Alex, for fighting with my father for you?" she asks.

"Look...." Alex tries to say but has no answer. What would he say? He

had never mentioned what he did for a living before he had brought her to his house. She had found out herself or rather time had shown her his true identity. One night he came home with a bullet in his arm. He was in pain, still he insisted upon not calling a doctor. Cathleen herself had to take the bullet out. He had slept off then. In the morning she asked him about the night before. And he told her about each and every aspect of his life.

He was actually a car-thief. Not only cars, he used to try his hands at almost any vehicle. From a very early age, since when his parents died in an accident, who were neither rich nor did they have much to give their son, he had learnt life's harsh ways. To live, he had to eat and to eat he needed money. So, for money he began stealing and selling the stolen items at any price. When he grew up a little more, he understood the job could be more promising, so he began stealing vehicles - starting with bicycles first. Then with onset of his twenties, he turned to motorcycles. He worked alone so he had no one to share the money. He also met a dealer who would give him fair price. Then he improved his skills and began stealing cars. The dealer was only too happy. The dealer, his people called him Bob, even gave him offer to work for him permanently but Alex remained a freelancer. But he gave the vehicles to Bob and no one else. So, this was the life of Alex. Free, money maker, a bachelor. And then he met Cathleen and everything changed. He loved her, but never told her about his job. The fear of losing her always gripped him. And that night when the police almost got him red-handed and a bullet pierced through his arm, he had no other option than to tell her.

"Even that day I had told you," says Cathleen now, "I should never have fought my father. I had told you I made the wrong choice."

"But you couldn't leave me," says Alex, "because you loved me. And I loved you too."

"That's why you left me instead." There is a pause as a loud rumble in

the clouds shake the very insides of the two.

***

"You know the conditions, Cathleen," says Alex, "I had promised you I would return..." He cannot complete the words. He is disturbed by a shadow passing right behind him. He turns to see only the cat. But there is something strange about it. It is standing at the door and staring at the couple. And suddenly it darts outside, perhaps in fear of something.

"And when? Alex," Cathleen says firmly, taking back Alex's attention, "you forgot to mention that."

Another clash of the clouds lightens up the faces of the two with the streak of lightening as the events that had led to their separation is once again crystal clear in front of their eyes. Cathleen had requested him to leave crime and take up a decent job. She would say they would leave the city, go some place else, but if they stayed here, Alex's grave would soon be dug. But Alex was not in the mood to give up. He would always go off singing whenever she began her nagging, or just shut her mouth with a kiss. She would just say, 'can't you grow up a little?' But destiny takes its turns alright. Cathleen got pregnant and fear for her child gave her a new strength. Once again she told him to leave the job, but when he didn't even listen, she broke the news to him. He was only too happy to realize he was going to be a father. They hadn't married yet and so she said, "not for me, Alex, but do it only for the child. I don't want to tell our child that his father lost his life while escaping from the police. That some damn bullet got into his head and took his life, please?" Alex kissed her forehead and said, "I will tell Bob today and then we will marry." She had hugged her tightest hug that day.

Bob was not a man to leave his allies so easily but when Alex said firmly, he didn't say anything. Alex just said, "look, Bob, this was my decision to do this job. And it will be my decision to leave it." These words fell like molten in Bob's ears. He gestured his men. Alex was hit on the head, grabbed and badly beaten. Then Bob took his face and said, "no one says 'no' to Bob, boy. You were wrong to think I would let you go that easily. Now, listen to me very carefully. I need vehicles. Alright? Cars. The most expensive ones, otherwise you know I can disappear you and that slut of yours and no one would even realize. But yes, I would disappear you first. I would make sure, before disappearing your lover, that she warms my bed." With this he was thrown out by his men.

Alex's eyes become firm with the thought. His fists are clenched. Totally broken, he had reached Cathleen after that and told the story. Both knew it was easy to get into the criminal world but it was as hard to get out of it. He can still clearly see the tears Cathleen's beautiful big eyes had dropped down her cheeks. The tears that had led him to take a decisive action against Bob.

***

After a long pause Alex says staring at Cathleen, "so what name did you think?"

"Name?"

"Yes, for the baby?" says Alex, looking around the room. Perhaps, he thinks she has given birth to the child. He clearly can't remember how long he was away. But he is hesitant to ask directly. Now he can hear whispers as well. But he cannot decide whether they are really whispers. Perhaps the wind? But then, he can see all the glass windows are locked. And now the door is closed as well. Only a minute ago the door was open when the cat had escaped. But now he realizes, how did the door open? He remembers clearly he had shut it while coming in, but when the cat stood at the door, it was half open. And now it is closed again. Is it really happening or is he having hallucinations, he cannot decide. Cathleen's undisturbed face confuses him more. She hasn't even bothered to notice. A tinge of fear downs over his face but he decides not to say anything to Cathleen now.

"You know how many months you were away?" she asks.

"Not so many months so as I can't take my child in my arms. Where's he... or is she a girl?"

Cathleen stares at him for some time. Then says, "do you know how it feels?"

"It feels what? What are you saying?" Alex is totally confused. Why is she talking like this instead of showing her the child?

"To be called a slut?" she bursts out suddenly with tears in her eyes, "to be called a whore. A concubine.... An unmarried mother, mistress of a criminal... the mother of a bast....a basta.." Her mouth is held by Alex and he wraps his arms around her. She has gone through too much. Her tears won't stop while he hushes her down. He has realized it wasn't easy for her - to bear a child, to be criticized by public, every day, every minute. People not talking to you, watching you with hateful eyes when you go out, as if you have done some kind of a sin. "People didn't accept me...even in the churc..." she can't complete her words. Her voice is broken due to the weeping. Alex had promised he would return as soon as possible after one last job. After this, he had promised, no one would bother them ever and they would be able to live happily with their child. But...he didn't return. He broke his promise.

***

"You know what happened that day when I left you for that last job?" says Alex. It seems necessary to him that she learns his story as well. Cathleen has put off with her crying. Her tears have dried. He had to cover his arms around her for a long time, to calm her down.

"Do I really need to know?" says Cathleen, a little hatred in her tone, "after all that has happened?"

Alex stares at her for a while and says, "yes. You need to know what happened." And thus he begins his story. That day after leaving, he went straight to the Community Hall. Bob's men were keeping an eye on him, so he couldn't do anything suspicious. He knew there was always police at the hall. He just had to go there and stand before them. He did exactly that. As soon as the officers saw him, they pulled out their guns and began moving towards him. The two men set by Bob to keep an eye on Alex, could understand his plan only when it was too late. They were standing across the road and they thought the police officers had seen them as well. So, they took out their weapons to shoot Alex down. As Alex had thought, there was a shootout and the two men were shot down by the cops. Alex took to hiding first, but when there was too much cross-fire, he took someone's car and sped off. The police followed. Everything was working as to his plan. Next, he would have to go to Bob's den. His lair was just beside the bus depot. Within half an hour Alex was there. He drove straight into Bob's lair with the police at his heels.

Chaos broke into Bob's lair as the men saw first the car enter and then the police jeep. The cops had already called for reinforcements as soon as they had entered the building and the firing had begun. Soon there were more sirens of police jeeps and the place got filled with gun-firing, injured, dead, and blood. Bob's empire was destroyed. But he had kept himself hidden and he had seen Alex hiding too. As soon as the arrests began Alex came out of his hiding place and started towards another exit. There was a smile on his face - of triumph, of joy, of the thought that he would love.... but suddenly something hit him on the back and he fell down. With his mind blacking out he could see Bob's angry face and a pistol in his hand. As his eyes closed he could hear more gun-fires and Bob's painful shriek......

"Oh," comes out of Cathleen's mouth. There is silence. Slowly her eyes well up and two drops fall down her cheeks.

"But now see, I am all fit and fine," says Alex, "I have returned. Everything's over."

"Yes, Alex," says she, "everything is really over."

Alex stares at Cathleen's face confused when he hears footsteps and the voices of two men from another room. One of them says, "c'mon, Jack, no one lives in this house. What the hell are you afraid of?" Alex tries to understand the meaning of what they are saying when the other man says, "yes, Paul, but I have heard it is haunted." Alex's confusions are explained by that single answer. He looks at Cathleen. And there is more. The man called Paul says again, "and I have heard we might still find something here, even 10 months after that slut of Alex killed herself." "What?" comes from Jack, "she was Alex's..." "Concubine, yes," says Paul, "what? You didn't know or what? Man, that dog Alex made some money after all and he had the hell of a beauty to warm his bed."

"Everything is really over, Alex," says Cathleen, her eyes watery, as

Alex stares at her in horror, "you are late." He puts his hands on his head. He has understood now the noise of breaking glass, the cat's escape and the unusual behavior of the door. The thieves are still inside, searching for something valuable. Tears fall down his cheeks. "Why?" he asks, "why?"

"Perhaps, I couldn't bear the jeers I had to listen every day," says Cathleen as calmly as before, "perhaps, I didn't want our child to go through all this. So, I just took in poison."

"And, our child?" asks Alex.

"Three months were still left for him to see the harsh world." Cathleen is calm. As if she is happy with what she did. She is satisfied.

Alex looks at her, then says, “I have something to show you. Will you come with me?”

***

It’s dawn. The sky is changing its color slowly. There is police in Cathleen’s house. They have found two dead bodies here. The assistant says to his officer, “when one of them called, he sounded very strange. He said he needed to be saved or else she would kill both of them. He said the witch had taken over his friend’s body and that he had done the biggest mistake of his life by coming here. When we reached here, we found them already dead.” The officer sighs and says, “do you know them?” The assistant nods his head and says, “Paul and Jack. They were just petty thieves.” The officer takes a heavy breathe and says, “another

death. Well, the fault is their own. They really shouldn’t have come here.”

The couple is standing in front of a grave. Cathleen’s face turns into a surprised one as she reads the name written on the tombstone. It’s written Alex Jackson. She then looks at Alex. “You know what?” says Alex, “that day when Bob shot me from behind, I had lost senses. When I woke up, there was no one in the small hospital room. I feared Bob was still alive and he would get to you next. I had to make sure you were safe. But just then I saw two men taking Bob’s dead body on a stretcher. I wanted to see him nicely but surprisingly the men didn’t notice me at all. I came back to my room and sat on the bed, disappointed. Just then I got the greatest horror of my life. My own body lay in front of me on the bed. Soon the doctor came in with an assistant. He was saying he felt sorry for me who died while I was brought to the hospital.”

Cathleen put her hand on his shoulder. “I couldn’t believe I was dead,” says Alex, “it took me some time to accept this fact and finally when the truth downed upon me I decided I still had work left. So, I came to you to tell you the truth, to meet you for the last time.”

“We are both on the same sides of the coin,” says Cathleen. Alex looks at her smiling face and sighs.

Today there were no rains. The water from yesterday night is drying slowly. The ground floor flat is glowing again but nobody cares to observe. It glows with the same fire beside which lie two naked bodies that have made love only moments ago. "You know what? I didn't want it to end this way," says Alex, taking Cathleen's palm in his, "at least you could have lived."

"At least we can be together now," says she and puts her other palm on his bare chest. Alex wraps his fingers around hers. Perhaps this is their destiny, he thinks, crime never pays, this is true. But now, yes, they can live happily in this forlorn quarter with no Bob or police to disturb them.

****

Printed by Libri Plureos GmbH in Hamburg,
Germany